Wel ome!

Dear Reader,

Welcome to a world of imagination!

My First Story was designed for Key Stage 1 children as an introduction to creative writing and to promote an enjoyment of reading and writing from an early age.

The simple, fun storyboards give even the youngest and most reluctant writers the chance to become interested in literacy by giving them a framework within which to shape their ideas. Pupils could also choose to write without the storyboards, allowing older children to let their creativity flow as much as possible, encouraging the use of imagination and descriptive language.

We believe that seeing their work in print will inspire a love of reading and writing and give these young writers the confidence to develop their skills in the future.

There is nothing like the imagination of children, and this is reflected in the creativity and individuality of the stories in this anthology. I hope you'll enjoy reading their first stories as much as we have.

Jenni Harrison

Editorial Manager

Imagine...

Each child could choose one of five storyboards, using the pictures and their imagination to create an exciting tale. You can view the storyboards at the end of this book.

There was also the option to create their own story using a blank template.

YORKSHIRE

CONTENTS

Dominik Gnas (7)	58
Colby Towler (7)	59
Dionne Everitt (7)	60
Aoife Monaghan (5)	61
Francesca Scholes (7)	62
Ruby Smith (7)	63
Joshua McLauchlan (7)	64
Milena Majcher (6)	65
Lucy Marsh (7)	66
Julian Rutkowski (6)	67
Charlie Gilbert (6)	68
Taylor James Sherburn (6)	69
Noah Simpson (6)	70
Joshua Akrill (5)	71
Harry Vaughan (6)	72
Tanner Towler (6)	73
Filip Truchan (6), Jessica & Pixi-Lil Sands Wright (6)	74
Shay Sands Wright (7)	75
Lewis Ward (6)	76
Angel Loynes (6)	77
Riley Parkin (6)	78
Nathan Addy Sherburn (6)	79
Layla Wassel (5)	80

Hoyle Court Primary School, Baildon

Ehsaan Asif (6)	81

IQRA Academy, Manningham

Hirah Mahmood (7)	82
Ahmed Mohamed Khaled Eldaly (7)	84
Talha Ali Khan (7)	86
Maryam Patel (6)	88
Misbah Inayah Ali (7)	90
Eiliyah Aftab (7)	91
Ali Irfan (7)	92
Sudais Khan (7)	93

New Bewerley Community School, Beeston

Iva Drevina (7)	94
Jainaba Drammeh (7)	95
Honey Allotey (7)	96
Anisa Quereshi (7)	97
Ismael Rahim (7)	98
Lily-Mai Simpson (7)	99
Louie Naylor (7)	100
Nickolas Lupu (7)	101

Oulton Primary School, Oulton

Freya Ann Winterbottom (6)	102
Lexi Rae Bruce (6)	103
Oscar Filip Shirripa (6)	104
Alana-Rose Rawson (6)	105
Lily P (6)	106

Ravenfield Primary Academy, Ravenfield

Paige Hope Ross (7)	107
Emily Woodcock (7)	108
Beau Lawton (6)	110
Isabell Davis (6)	112
Katie Wood (7)	113
Theo Priestley (7)	114
James Wood (7)	115
Bobby Parkin (7)	116
Alexia Wild (7)	117
Rubi Zahir (7)	118
Rohan Gray (7)	119
Reece Ramskill (7)	120
Summer Rose Muffett (6)	121
Darcey Beth Allsop (7)	122
Sophie Needle (7)	123
Eden Grace Ross (7)	124
Charlotte Mary Sanderson (6)	125
Archie Ridley (7)	126
James Wharin (7)	127
Cruz Lee Pearce (7)	128
Sophia Lucy Wagstaff (6)	129
Oliver Patrick Wild (7)	130

Charlie Hobson (7)	131
Sadie Wharton (7)	132
Ben Saville (7)	133
Harry Thewlis (7)	134
Alfie Whitehouse (7)	135

Southroyd Primary School, Pudsey

Lucy Anne Rose (7)	136
Aimee Rose Hunt (7)	137
Mia Hemingway (7)	138
Pippa-Rose Keough (5)	139
Harleen Panesar (6)	140
Toby James Grayson (7)	141
Adam Tasker (6)	142
Autumn Isabelle McDonald (6)	143
Jaden Thiara (6)	144
Maisy Summer Crowther (6)	145
Lewie Ambler (5)	146

St Nicholas Primary School, Hull

Angela (Yuan Yuan) Huang (5)	147
Violet Wilkinson (5)	148
Faith Dixon (5)	149
Robbie West (4)	150

The Forest School, Knaresborough

Liam Mpholle (7)	151

Tranmoor Primary School, Armthorpe

Libby Louise Aston (7)	152
Lexi Challis (7)	155
Leah Nicholson (7)	156
Katelyn Foers (7)	158
Lucas Philip Cowley (6)	160
Kacie-Jayne Birtles (7)	162
Olivia Jane Watkinson (7)	164
Flynn White (7)	165
Ava Rose Barrass (7)	166
Bradley Wehrle (7)	167

Niall Nevin (7)	168
Harry Walker (7)	169
Mason Walker (6)	170
Fletcher Elden (7)	171
Faith Doherty (7)	172
Flynn Broome (6)	173
James Grey (7)	174
Dylan Marshall (7)	175

West End Academy, Hemsworth

Elaina-Mai Petch (5)	176
Ivy Clough (5)	177
Holly Camponi (5)	178
Kye Julian Stogden (5)	179

Woodlands CE Primary School, Woodlands

Megan Pearson (7)	180
Harry Mitchell (6)	182
Austin Wade (7)	183
Lily Ford (7)	184
Eva Lee (6)	185
Olivia Brooke Atkins (7)	186
Isabelle Johnson (6)	187
Scarlet Tempest (6)	188
Rosie Elizabeth Swift (7)	189
James Turkmen Holmes (7)	190

The Stories

Maryam's Jungle Story

Emma and Ben swung in the trees. They met a snake. They felt scared! Emma and Ben were feeling scared, so Emma and Ben ran away from the snake.

Emma and Ben met a lion and the lion was friendly. The lion took them on a ride. Emma and Ben were so happy.

Maryam Kelendar

The Dinosaurs

When I was walking in a dark forest, I came by a time machine, so I sat on it and pushed the lever to the past and it made a crashing noise.

When I got there, I didn't know where I was. I reached a big bad dinosaur and knew I was at Dinosaur's Land and I found a cosy place to sleep. Soon, when I woke up, in front of me was an allosaurus staring at me, but it was friendly and let me on its back to see tall trees, muddy bits and an amazing stream.

Soon after that, I came by some eggs. Their mum wasn't there. The white eggs were all alone, so I looked after them. Soon, I got tired so I went to sleep.

But when I woke up, their mum was there, but one shiny white egg did not hatch so their mum was chasing me.

Soon I had to go, so I sat on the time machine and it still made a crash noise when I pushed it to the present. I got home and I went to bed, but a dinosaur followed me...

Leah Owen (7)
Brompton-On-Swale CE Primary School, Brompton-On-Swale

Emma And The Dinosaurs!

Once upon a time, there was a girl called Emma. She wanted to go to the museum, so she went. She saw a time machine. The arrow was switching to the past...

She got there after ten hours of driving. There were volcanoes, geysers and dinosaurs. It was scary and magnificent!

After that, she saw a colossal T-rex. She wanted to go, but the T-rex said, "Hi."

"Hi," she said. "My name is Emma."

"My name is Dan."

As Emma walked along, she saw an egg, and another and another. Three eggs. One of them had a crack. One, two three, they all were cracked! Emma tried to climb the tree, but she couldn't climb it so she looked up and she could see their mum shouting at her. She didn't mind, but she decided to go home.

She got on her time machine and went home and ran up to her dad then her mum. After a long day, she went to bed.

Gracie-Mai Simpson (7)

Brompton-On-Swale CE Primary School, Brompton-On-Swale

An Extraordinary Adventure

First, Alice and Rose sat on a time machine that their dad made and pulled the lever to the past. Sparks came up and the time machine went *bang, crash, thump!*

And they went to the land of the dinosaurs! They saw flexible dinosaurs, bad-tempered dinosaurs, but one dinosaur was sad and they went to talk to it.

Then the king, T-Rex, was spying on them because the sad dinosaur found something he wanted and he was the king.

T-Rex came out and said, "Drop that now!" but she said no.

The girls saw some eggs. They went to them. A dinosaur tried to eat them, but they stopped the dinosaur.

The girls saw a dinosaur going to put the eggs in a cave.

Finally, they sat on the time machine and went home.

Alice Rhodes (7)

Brompton-On-Swale CE Primary School, Brompton-On-Swale

A Magical Adventure

First I went on a walk with my dog and found a new shiny time machine that someone had lost, so me and my dog sat on it and it took me to the land of dinosaurs.

Then, when we landed in the world of dinosaurs, we saw some huge ones. We saw no dinosaurs in the deep water, so I found a stick and threw it in the deep water.

Jake Rex tried to eat me because he was hungry and was looking for food. Jake Rex found a small person to take back to his babies.

Then some more dinosaurs hatched and then they had a fight and then they stopped fighting and fed their babies.

The pterodactyl flew to get Jake.

"I'm home, I'm finally home!" I took my time machine to my bedroom and I had a disco.

Jake Ethan Bramley Foster (7)
Brompton-On-Swale CE Primary School, Brompton-On-Swale

Dino World

Once upon a time, there was a time machine. I pulled the lever and sat down, then it took me to Dino World!

When I got there, there was lots of sand, trees, dinosaurs, volcanoes and a beautiful sky and white clouds.

Then I went to the museum and looked at the dinosaur bones. They were shiny white and lovely shapes.

Then there were dinosaurs and big flying dinosaurs. One hatched and started to chase me and I started screaming!

They could fly, I couldn't. That wasn't fair! Dinosaurs couldn't speak, so I wasn't going to speak to them. They had scaly tails.

At last, I got back to the time machine. It was scary. I told my mum I was getting rid of it and would never get it back.

Lexi Horner (7)
Brompton-On-Swale CE Primary School, Brompton-On-Swale

Isla's Adventure

Isla was sitting on the time machine. The lever quickly turned to the past and it went back to the dinosaurs!

Then she looked around and there were dinosaurs everywhere! She was getting scared, so she was starting to get faster and faster.

Then she stopped and hid behind the bushes and she saw a Tyrannosaurus rex and an allosaurus fighting, then she saw a velociraptor flying to reach some eggs.

However, Isla scooped the eggs up. The dinosaur was mad, so he flew as fast as he could to get the eggs! He was going so fast that he was getting slower and slower...

The girl sat on the time machine and turned the lever to the present. Finally, she got home.

Isla Egan (7)
Brompton-On-Swale CE Primary School, Brompton-On-Swale

Dinosaur World

I was in a museum and I was looking at a time machine, then I accidentally knocked the glass and smashed it! I thought I would get told off, but I realised there was no one around, so I jumped on. It really did take you to the world of dinosaurs! I was walking in the deep green jungle and I walked past a T-rex, then it chased me and I ran. Then, whilst I was running, I saw a tree to climb up. Then, when I was at the tippy-top of the tree, I saw some eggs! But then the mum pterodactyl swooped down and the T-rex saw it. Now it knew where I was hiding and then they both started to chase me. Now I really ran! I led them to the time machine...

Isabelle Tyreman (7)
Brompton-On-Swale CE Primary School, Brompton-On-Swale

The Dinosaur Story

Once upon a time, there lived a pterodactyl and the pterodactyl found a time machine. She stepped inside and went to Dinosaur Land.

Then when she got there, she saw a volcano and dinosaurs eating grass and she found some eggs and the pterodactyl thought they were hers. She swooped down and got them, but then they hatched.

Then she realised they weren't hers, so she panicked and then she flew up into the clouds. Then she was still panicking because the dinosaur that the eggs belonged to came!

And then she went back into the time machine and went back to the past and lived happily ever after.

Katie Heron (7)

Brompton-On-Swale CE Primary School, Brompton-On-Swale

The Scary Story

I was walking my dog and when I came back I saw a time machine! I sat on it and it took me to a place that had lots of dinosaurs. I didn't know where I was!

I saw a dinosaur and it came up to me. I was scared. I was walking slowly. I saw another dinosaur, so I ran as fast as I could.

I saw a dinosaur. I hid behind it so it couldn't see me.

I saw some eggs in a nest. I watched them. I was bored, so I walked off.

I saw a dinosaur. I sat on it and it flew back to the time machine.

Finally, I sat on the time machine and it took me home. I got in my pyjamas and got in my bed.

Chloe Hanratty (6)
Brompton-On-Swale CE Primary School, Brompton-On-Swale

Ava's Dinosaur Adventure

First, Ava went to the museum and she found a time machine! She got on it and pulled the lever and she went to the past. There were volcanoes with red lava and long wavy grass. There were loud stomps on the ground.

A dinosaur heard Ava in the damp, cold bush. Then it was chasing her, but she saw a hiding spot and found some eggs. They were going to hatch. Just then, a pterodactyl came. Two eggs hatched! The pterodactyl swooped down and sat on the eggs. Ava ran to the time machine and pulled the level and *whoosh!* She was gone. She was tired and went to bed.

Ava Craggs (7)
Brompton-On-Swale CE Primary School, Brompton-On-Swale

The Special Story

Once, I was walking my dog and there was a time machine. I sat on it and it took me to a different place.
When I got to the place, it had damp grass and trees and dinosaurs. I got scared, but a T-rex came up to me.
But the T-rex nearly ate me because she was hungry and she liked people.
Then I carried on walking and I saw some eggs and they were in a nest.
And then I looked up and there was a different dinosaur flying up in the sky.
Finally, I got home and I went to bed and it was late. It was painful and I didn't know what happened.

Jorja Knights (7)
Brompton-On-Swale CE Primary School, Brompton-On-Swale

Dinosaur Land

One day I was walking to the park and I saw a time machine. I got into it and turned the lever. It turned to the past.

With a *pop!* I saw lots and lots of dinosaurs. There was a stegosaurus and some T-rexes. They were my favourite.

Then I saw another T-rex! It saw me. It was chasing me. It was roaring and roaring, then I finally lost it!

Then I saw some eggs on a tree. A velociraptor sat on the eggs and they hatched.

The T-rex came back and I was running and running and I got in the time machine.

Yes! I got home.

Emmie Lambert (7)
Brompton-On-Swale CE Primary School, Brompton-On-Swale

The Dinosaur Park

I found a time travel machine. I sat on it and went super fast into the past. I bumped into some dinosaurs when I got to Dinosaur World.
Then I saw a massive dinosaur! His name was Meat Eater. I ran away from him into a cave.
In the cave, I saw some dinosaur eggs lying there. A pterodactylus came flying in with his sharp claws and wanted to take me away from his nest.
I jumped out of the nest and ran to the machine. I quickly got back in the machine and travelled back home where I was safe.

Oliver Jones (7)
Brompton-On-Swale CE Primary School, Brompton-On-Swale

The Boy And The Dinosaurs

Somebody sat on the chair and twisted the handle. He was called Danny. He was wanting to see a dinosaur.

He arrived! He was excited because he saw a T-rex. Danny was happy.

Danny saw a dinosaur that had sharp teeth and it was big.

Danny saw some eggs and Danny carefully went around the eggs.

Danny saw a pterodactyl was flying in the air. It was circling Danny.

Danny rushed home and ran in the house. He was terrified! He hid in his bed.

Elliott Tobias Hindmarch (6)

Brompton-On-Swale CE Primary School, Brompton-On-Swale

The Dinosaur Story

In my back garden there was a time machine. I sat on it, then I pulled it to the past.

Then it took me to a dinosaur place and the dinosaurs caught me there.

Rose Rex tried to eat me because she was hungry and looking for food, but Rose Rex found a small person to eat.

Then a pterodactyl flew up to get the eggs. The pterodactyl flew to get Rose.

I ran to the time machine, then I pulled it to present to go home.

Rose Harris (7)

Brompton-On-Swale CE Primary School, Brompton-On-Swale

Josh Is In Jurassic Park

The funky machine could take you to the past, present or future and all you needed to do was flick the lever!

We went to the dinosaur age. The volcanic volcano erupted. I saw a T-rex hiding in the leaves with sharp teeth and claws.

The velociraptor's nest was in the trees. A flying velociraptor flew in the clouds.

Finally, I got home. I lay in bed and went to sleep.

Josh Reed (6)

Brompton-On-Swale CE Primary School, Brompton-On-Swale

T-Rex

Ava sat on the time machine. It was scary. She spun around the lever and went to the past.
It looked like the land of the dinosaurs. She saw a volcano and two small blue and red dinosaurs. There was a T-rex that crept up to a pterodactyl and ate it up! Ava ran away.
When she was running away, she saw a nest with three pterodactyl eggs in it...

George Whitaker (6)
Brompton-On-Swale CE Primary School, Brompton-On-Swale

The Adventure Of A Dinosaur

One day, I found a time machine. I got on the time machine and went to the past.

I crashed into a diplodocus. There was a volcano and lava.

I heard a dinosaur looking for his nest of fossils. I found some of his eggs and the eggs were fossils. Then the pterodactylus scooped me up!

Finally, I went home and had a cup of tea.

Heather Jade Twyman (7)

Brompton-On-Swale CE Primary School, Brompton-On-Swale

Amazing

Ava found a time machine in the woods. She jumped in and sat down. She pulled the lever to the past.

She banged her head by landing on a dinosaur, Spike. Ava patted him on his nose.

A hungry T-rex was stomping through the bushes. He was once a person. A wizard had cast a spell on him...

Micah Francis (7)

Brompton-On-Swale CE Primary School, Brompton-On-Swale

The Shape-Shifter

A boat far away was paddling across the ocean.
Swoop! The wind turned the boat over!
The shape-shifter turned into a seahorse. Next, he turned into a shark. The shark had sharp teeth and blue, sharp, pointy shark fins.
Next, the shark met a mermaid and the mermaid said hello.
Then the mermaid met a man mermaid called Ryan. He had a red tail like the little mermaid's hair.
The lady mermaid had a little wave. Her tail was magic and gave the shape-shifter's legs back. He paddled back to the shore.

Sian Conway (7)

Headlands Primary School, Haxby

In The Jungle

In a jungle, dark, scary and creepy creatures live. There is a green poisonous snake with sharp teeth and mysterious eyes and it kills teachers at Headlands School. It has a long tongue as red as fire and it could bite your finger off with its sharp teeth.

There is a scary and ferocious lion rushing through the reeds. He starts to run and he leaps a bit until he finds a snake's home. He decides to eat the snake, but the snake is poisonous, so when he goes into the house, he gets killed by the snake.

Matthew Moore (7)
Headlands Primary School, Haxby

The Dragon And The Unicorn

One sunny day, a rainbow appeared above a castle. The pillars were green and the roof was light pink.

Just then, a dragon trotted by. He turned his head at the castle. As soon as he saw this, he approached it. The dragon tried to burn it down! But...

A unicorn ran by and made friends with him! Then they held hands gently.

Dragon said, "It's time for me to go."

Unicorn said, "Okay."

Soon, Unicorn went home to sleep.

Niamh Louisa Dixon (7)

Headlands Primary School, Haxby

The Little Unicorns

Once upon a time, there was a unicorn castle. A dragon came stomping over to the castle.
The dragon said, "Where is the princess unicorn?"
One unicorn said, "She is in here."
The dragon burnt down the castle. The princess unicorn didn't know because she was asleep.
The princess unicorn said, "Hello."
The dragon said hello back.
The dragon said bye and the unicorn said bye.
The unicorn went back home and they lived happily ever after.

Mia Stevens (6)
Hill Top CE Primary School, Low Moor

The Robo Alien

Once upon a time, there lived an astronaut. He crashed and bashed and landed on a spaceship. He saw a space creature taking his rocket.
"Where is this? I think it's a spaceship. There's a space crash! Oh no, my rocket! Give me my rocket back!" said the astronaut.
"No, never, don't come back!" said the alien.
"I need to get my rocket back!" said the astronaut.
"I will kill you!" the space creature said. He killed him.

Thomas Pedder (6)
Hill Top CE Primary School, Low Moor

A Space Tale

Once upon a time, there was a boy called James. It was his dream to go to the moon. When James was thirty-two, he could finally go to the moon. On the moon, James was not alone. Out of the shadows came the fiercest, kindest alien.

"Can I be your friend?" James said. "My ship is broken."

The alien said, "Yes, I see that."

James said, "Sooo, can you fix it?"

"Listen kid, I left that life behind me," said the alien.

Henry Garry (6)

Hill Top CE Primary School, Low Moor

A Space Adventure

Once upon a time, a boy went to space. He went in a rocket. He went to the moon. He had a picnic on the moon. He saw some stars and Earth.
He saw a spaceship. He looked inside the spaceship and he saw an alien. They had a picnic with each other. They made friends. They played with each other, but the boy had to go and the alien said goodbye.
Then the alien had to go. They both went home. They both had their tea. They both went to bed.

Amelia Jade Davies (6)
Hill Top CE Primary School, Low Moor

Katie's Under The Sea Story

Once, there was a boat. The boat sank.
A crab saw a fish. The crab asked, "Are you lost?"
"Yes," replied the fish.
Then a shark came along. It was big and it had big sharp teeth.
Ariel came and her father came out and they scared the shark away.
Then Ariel and her dad had a dance party and all the animals joined in too.
Then they gave each other gifts, then everyone lived happily ever after.

Katie Preston (6)
Hill Top CE Primary School, Low Moor

A Unicorn Tale

Once upon a time, there was a rainbow unicorn in a castle. She was a baby unicorn. In fact, she was a little baby. She was cute!

The dragon was scaring the cute baby rainbow unicorn.

The dragon was making a fire on the unicorn castle, but the dragon was trying to be nice. They shook hands.

The unicorn said, "Bye!"

The dragon said, "Bye!"

The unicorn was crying.

The unicorn went back home.

Fareeha Hussain (6)
Hill Top CE Primary School, Low Moor

Little Unicorns

Once, there was a castle. Inside it, there were two unicorns. One of them was a baby.
A dragon came along and breathed all over the castle!
"Argh!" said Mum. "Quick, get out of the house!"
The house burnt down.
"Where are we going to live now?" said Mum.
The unicorn was friends with the dragon. The dragon flew away.
"Bye!" said the unicorn.
They found a new home.

Paygan Jade Turner (6)
Hill Top CE Primary School, Low Moor

Space Story

There was a little boy who loved space. He asked his mum if he could go to space.

His mum said, "Yes, of course."

He got a box. He got some toys. He saw a rocket and an alien popped out!

The alien said hello. The little boy said hello back to the alien. The little boy was shy.

The boy was friends with the alien, so he had dinner with him. They went to the alien's house and had dinner and went to bed.

Lilly Rose Mary Shaw (6)

Hill Top CE Primary School, Low Moor

The Story Of The Scary Shark

The boat sank into the water.

The crab came up to the boat. Fishes swam around and the crab was looking at the fishes.

A shark came and smiled. The crab hid from the shark. The shark was hungry.

The king and the princess scared away the shark.

The king and princess were happy because they scared the shark away.

The king and the princess lifted the boat back up.

The crab went back down in the water.

Mason Martin Grange (6)

Hill Top CE Primary School, Low Moor

The Aliens On Earth

Once upon a time, a rocket flew. It flew to Earth.
When the rocket got there, the boy got out.
When he got out, he saw a goblin.
The goblin got out of its flying saucer. The boy said hello. The goblin said hello.
The goblin took the rocket to the alien planet. The boy got out and said hello.
The goblins said, "Do you want to have a party?"
He said, "Yes!"

Reggie Lee Murch (6)

Hill Top CE Primary School, Low Moor

Ashleigh's Magical Story

Once upon a time, there lived a unicorn. There was a castle and the unicorn lived there.

Just at that moment, a dragon arrived. He said, "I am lost," to the unicorn.

The dragon got angry and breathed fire on the castle.

The unicorn and dragon became friends. The unicorn and dragon said goodbye and the dragon flew away.

The unicorn went home and lived happily ever after.

Ashleigh Francesca Chisato (6)
Hill Top CE Primary School, Low Moor

Harveer's Space Story

Once, a man was scared of blast-off. It was time to go. He was brave and he went in the spaceship. He met another ship. The man's petrol ran out, so the alien took him to space and he landed. He met another alien but it was a nice one. They played and played and played.

Then they had a picnic and played. He met some more aliens, a hundred or two hundred aliens.

He went back home.

Harveer Dhillon (6)

Hill Top CE Primary School, Low Moor

Unicorns

Once upon a time, there was a beautiful land called Unicorn Land.
They then heard a big storm in Unicorn Land. Then a dragon scraped the castle with his claws! He breathed fire all over the castle.
The mummy unicorn said, "Come out, come out!"
Then, with her magic, she blew him away! He flew away. He never came back again.
They lived happily ever after!

Holly Farooq (6)
Hill Top CE Primary School, Low Moor

A Space Adventure

Once upon a time, there was a rocket.
It crash-landed on the moon.
There was a spaceship flying around in space.
An alien said, "Hello!" and the boy said hello back.
They became friends.
The alien picked up the rocket and one of the
rocket's legs fell off!
The alien took the boy home in his spaceship. They
mended the rocket.

Joel Ruben Illingworth (6)
Hill Top CE Primary School, Low Moor

A Unicorn Tale

Once upon a time, there was a unicorn.
It lived in a castle next to a rainbow.
Then one day, a dragon came. He stood outside
and he waited for the unicorn to come out. He
blew fire at the castle, until the unicorn came out.
The unicorn made friends with the dragon, then
the dragon went into the sky.
The unicorn lived happily ever after.

Daisy Beau Chancellor (5)
Hill Top CE Primary School, Low Moor

The Mermaid

Once upon a time, there was a little boy. He went fishing.

He fell into the water. He found a crab.

The boy screamed because he met a shark!

The boy met a mermaid. It was very noisy.

Her dad came. He said, "What are you doing out here? It's dangerous!"

They went back home. They lived happily ever after.

Emelia Sutcliffe (5)

Hill Top CE Primary School, Low Moor

A Unicorn Tale

Once upon a time, there lived a unicorn in a castle and there was a rainbow.
A scary dragon came to the castle. He shouted, "Unicorn, come out right now!"
The scary dragon blew fire on the castle.
They became friends forever. The dragon flew away.
The unicorn went back home happily ever after.

Inayah Iqbal (6)
Hill Top CE Primary School, Low Moor

A Space Tale

Once upon a time, a rocket flew to space. A rocket flew to Earth. It was his dream.
There was an alien invasion and a spaceship. In space, there were stars.
An alien came and said, "Hiya!"
The rocket crashed into the spaceship.
The spaceship went back to space. They lived happily ever after.

Barron James Fisher (7)
Hill Top CE Primary School, Low Moor

Harvey's Space Story

Once upon a time, there was a little astronaut. He went into space in a puff of smoke.
He saw Earth and landed on the moon. There were stars.
He saw an alien spaceship.
He saw an alien waving and laughing at him.
The alien then beamed up a rocket.
The alien took the astronaut back home.

Harvey Dewhurst (5)
Hill Top CE Primary School, Low Moor

Under The Sea

Once, there was a boat on the sea.

Under the water, there were sea creatures.

One day a fierce shark came.

The pretty mermaid said, "Help, help!" and her dad rescued her.

The pretty mermaid was safe.

The pretty mermaid went up to the surface with her dad.

Ellah Stajkowski (6)

Hill Top CE Primary School, Low Moor

A Space Adventure

The boy went in the spaceship. The boy flew to the moon. He had lunch at the moon. The boy saw the stars.

The boy went in a different spaceship. The boy saw an alien!

The boy got scared. The alien's spaceship broke! The boy's spaceship brought it home.

Charlie White (6)

Hill Top CE Primary School, Low Moor

Alien Invasion

Once upon a time, there was a little spaceship.
It flew around the world.
It was a shiny spinning spaceship.
An alien with three eyes said, "Hi!"
A rocket crashed into the spaceship!
The big spaceship and the rocket flew home.

Jack Patrick Michael Jardine (6)

Hill Top CE Primary School, Low Moor

The Deep, Dark Jungle

Once upon a time in a deep dark jungle, there lived black and white snakes. They loved to creep up on people, except for one snake called Shimon. He was the bravest snake of all, but he was scared of one thing: a lion!

One day, Shimon decided to have a little trip around the jungle. Every other snake thought that it was a bad idea because there could be a lion out there. They tried to shout, "There will be a lion out there!" but he wouldn't listen to them.

Halfway into the darkest piece of the jungle, he turned into a lion! He was running, but he turned into a snake again! He landed with a *bump!* He hurt himself really badly and he was bleeding because of glass in him.

Shimon turned back into a lion and he was scared of himself! Whilst Shimon was looking in the closest river, he got used to being a lion. Especially being king!

It felt *amazing!* Shimon did a gargantuan roar! "*Roar!*" He ran off to the other snakes and said, "Hello, I am Shimon... don't be afraid!"

Everybody hid.

He ran everywhere. He realised he couldn't find other lions. He was all by himself.

He was growing up bravely with nobody there with him.

Eventually, he had a wife and ninety-two children. He was brave and strong, so he taught them very well. The family went on and on forever. They lived happily ever after.

Amelia Jayne Baker-Richardson (7)
Holy Family & St Michael's Catholic Primary School, Pontefract

A Scary Shark Is Scared Of A Mermaid

In the middle of the deep clear ocean, there was an old boat floating around. The rusty boat was going from one side to another. No one knew where it came from.

Under the ocean, there was a little cute crab who was leaving the ocean. He was saying goodbye to his wonderful friends under the ocean.

Deep down in the dark ocean, there lived a mean shark who did not like the little crab. He was trying not to be scared of a mermaid. It looked like he was not shy, but he actually was very shy.

The shark was too shy around the cute and beautiful mermaid. Then the mermaid king swam to scare the mean shark. Sometimes the shark was even scared of the grey fin on the end of his body.

It was time for the crab to leave the ocean. Little Mermaid decided to make a leaving party for the little crab, who was a little bit sad and excited. The little mermaid and the king waved goodbye to the little crab.

The crab said, "I can't wait to make new wonderful friends!" with a big smile on his face.

Adrianna Majcher (8)
Holy Family & St Michael's Catholic Primary School, Pontefract

The Magical Mermaid!

Once upon a time, there was a girl called Sabreana. Sabreana was sailing to a desert. But then there was a mermaid called Ava and she turned Sabreana into a mermaid!

Sabreana asked, "What did you do?"

"Ha, ha, ha! Do you like it? I'm Alia."

Sabreana sang, "Under the sea is a magical place, I'm the most magical mermaid in the world and in the sea..."

"Oh no! There is a shark! It's coming!" said Alia.

"Okay now," said Sabreana. "Shoo, shoo! If you don't shoo, there will be trouble!"

"Okay then," said the shark.

"Good," said Sabreana.

"Thank you!" said Alia.

"You're welcome! Alia, can we dance?"

"Yes, sure!"

"Under the sea is a magical place, under the sea..."

Later...

"Bye, I will see you soon!"

"Hmm, okay, but are you sure?"

"Yes, now bye!"

Simona Todorova Lyubenova (7)

Holy Family & St Michael's Catholic Primary School, Pontefract

The Dinosaur World!

One day, something huge dropped on Earth and a beautiful bird came by. He flew down to the huge machine and it pressed a button on the huge machine.

The machine went *boom!* three times! Somehow, it teleported the bird to Jurassic Park and there was a beautiful dinosaur. There was a huge volcano full of boiling hot lava.

When he was walking around, he saw a huge T-rex hunting for its prey. It was super-duper scary. Also, the T-rex looked him straight in the eyes, but he thought he might take a picture of it.

After he saw the T-rex, he wanted to climb a tree and look at the view. When he finally got to the top of the tree, he saw three eggs and he actually saw one hatch!

The dinosaur grew bigger and bigger. He tried to teach it how to fly, which he did!

He finally got tired as he'd had a long day at Jurassic Park, so he went home and he saw a dinosaur. It lived with him forever.

Summary Grace Mellor (7)

Holy Family & St Michael's Catholic Primary School, Pontefract

The Loudest Dinosaur

Once upon a time, a man called Steven went into his basement and he went into his time machine and he saw a T-rex and stegosaurus.

Steven saw a huge volcano, it was erupting! He nearly died, but Steven outran the lava. All the dinosaurs were running away too, but one was hurt! Steven was a medic, so he could hear it.

Steven saw a T-rex. It was eating a raptor. It was so smelly! It saw Steven. It was going to eat Steven! He outran the T-rex, he was very lucky.

A stegosaurus laid three huge eggs. After thirty-four days, they hatched and the mother dino got them a red pterodactyl so they grew into teenagers.

Steven rode on a pterodactyl back to the time machine and a T-rex followed him to the time machine. The dinosaur got on the back.

He went back to the present day. When he got home, he had a pet dinosaur. It was an extremely bad dinosaur!

Joe Harrison (7)
Holy Family & St Michael's Catholic Primary School, Pontefract

The Dragon Who Turned Friendly

One day in a far, faraway land, there was a shining rainbow on top of a magical castle with an enchanted magical tree. Magicorn was really lucky to live in the castle.

One day, a fearsome dragon named Rex flew to the castle. He wanted to destroy Magicorn's castle. Rex landed on a smooth hill. He was feeling very angry and with his mighty fire he set the castle on fire.

Magicorn looked out the window and thought, *what's happening?* She rushed to the dragon and said, "Who are you?" She knew she had to stop him.

Magicorn used her special powers to turn him into a friendly dragon and sent him into the misty clouds.

"What a day!" she said. "I might need a rest."

She trotted down the lane to her new castle. She lived happily ever after.

Sophia Grace Ponsonby (6)

Holy Family & St Michael's Catholic Primary School, Pontefract

The Dragon And Unicorn

Once upon a time, there lived a unicorn called Charlotte. She lived in a castle with a dragon flying around it.

One day, the unicorn looked out of the window and then she went outside and she saw the dragon. She went inside because she was scared. The dragon saw Charlotte go in the castle. The dragon went to the window and he breathed fire and said, "Hello."

Charlotte saw him out of the window, so she went outside again. They had a look at each other and held each other's hands.

Then the dragon was showing Charlotte that he could fly and she said, "Could you teach me to fly?"

"Yes, I will," said the dragon.

Then she said, "Goodbye, I will see you tomorrow!" She went home happy because she had a new friend.

Evie Butler (6)

Holy Family & St Michael's Catholic Primary School, Pontefract

The Mermaid Rescue

One beautiful day, the waves were a tiny bit big and there was an old empty boat on the sea and the birds were flying in the sky
Under the water there were some wonderful creatures, even a dancing crab who was funny! There was a lot of seaweed.
The next day, the most fierce shark ever was very hungry. His name was Sharky. He scared all the animals into their hiding places.
Behind Sharky appeared Coral and Kingy, and Kingy was going to poke his bum to scare him away!
All the mermaids celebrated! They were happy and all the animals were happy as well. Everyone was playing their favourite music.
They found a boat and they got in it and sailed to the other side so there were no terrible creatures.

India Armstrong (6)

Holy Family & St Michael's Catholic Primary School, Pontefract

Magic Dinosaurs

Once upon a time, there was a machine and it took a boy to the past with the dinosaurs. He heard a roar, it was a T-rex! It was fighting with another dinosaur, a triceratops. The boy ran away.

The T-rex was following him. He kept running and running. At last, he lost it. He found a man who was called Joe and he was hunting dinosaurs.

The next day, they saw some eggs in a nest and they were going to see what they were. They could have been dinosaur eggs or bird eggs.

Suddenly, the mum came to the nest. Joe was hunting it down, then it started to rain a lot and they got the dinosaur down.

The time machine took the boy back home. Joe was still in the past, still hunting for dinosaurs...

Charlie David Thomas (6)

Holy Family & St Michael's Catholic Primary School, Pontefract

The Little Lion

Once upon a time, there was a little lion. He lived with loads of different lions. Those lions had a very difficult life. They wanted to live in a different place.

A snake was looking for dinner. He found a little lion. It was his dinner. He tried to catch the little lion, but he couldn't catch him! He tried everything, but nothing happened.

The lion was too good and too clever and too fast, so the snake said, "No, no, no, this is no good! I will have a little lion for my dinner, but not today."

The little lion was still running, but then it saw that the snake was not chasing him. The little lion saw a place and other lions were there. He was happy, so he ran to them.

Emilia Kapustka (7)
Holy Family & St Michael's Catholic Primary School, Pontefract

Space Adventure

Once upon a time, there lived a man called Steve. He was a spaceman. He was in his rocket and he was close to landing the rocket. Finally, he landed on the moon. He then went out of the rocket. After that, he walked a bit.

Then he heard a noise, so he looked in the air and an alien was flying and it landed. He saw the friendly alien. He took him to the rocket and gave him some alien food, then Steve lived with him. But then the wings broke off the rocket, so the alien went in his space rocket and stuck the wing back.

Steve tried to take off, but it fell down. Then something bad happened! The rocket went down and Steve crashed! People came and called the ambulance.

Dominik Gnas (7)

Holy Family & St Michael's Catholic Primary School, Pontefract

T-Rex Adventures

Once upon a time, a boy called Dash made a time machine that went into the past, present and future. Once, he tested it out and went into the past.

When he got there, Dash got out of the time machine and it broke! When he looked behind himself, he saw a T-rex. He ran away as fast as he could and, when he looked behind himself again, it was gone.

Then he saw a tree with eggs in and he climbed up the tree and he said, "T-rex won't find me now!" Then he saw a pteranodon and it grabbed him! He tried to get out of his claws and he did and landed on a brachiosaurus. He was right back at the start and he fixed the time machine and went back home.

Colby Towler (7)

Holy Family & St Michael's Catholic Primary School, Pontefract

The Unicorn And Dragon

Once upon a time, there was a dragon and a unicorn. They were fighting together. They were fighting because the dragon stole the unicorn's magic. That was how they got in that horrible fight! The unicorn got the dragon down, but the dragon got up.

The dragon got really angry because the unicorn pushed the dragon again.

The unicorn said, "Shoo, shoo! If you don't shoo, I will steal *your* magic."

They both got tired, but they were still fighting together.

The dragon said, "Ha ha ha! You will never get the magic!"

The dragon needed to go, so the unicorn tip-tapped home. The unicorn family went to sleep.

Dionne Everitt (7)

Holy Family & St Michael's Catholic Primary School, Pontefract

The Mermaid Rescue

One lovely beautiful day, the sea was nice and calm with an empty boat floating along.

Under the water there was a dancing crab and lots of fish swimming in the water. They were feeling happy.

One day, Sharky was very hungry and he went to find the sea animals to eat them, but they all went into their hiding spaces.

Behind Sharky appeared Coral and Kingy with his weapon fork to poke Sharky's bum and scare him away.

Coral and Kingy and the other sea animals were celebrating and dancing and shouting while the shark went away very sad.

Coral and Kingy went to the top of the blue sea and went into the boat and went to Mermaid Land.

Aoife Monaghan (5)

Holy Family & St Michael's Catholic Primary School, Pontefract

Under The Clear Ocean

In the middle of the clear ocean, there was an old rusty boat floating around in circles. The boat was going from one side to the other.
Under the sparkling ocean was a smiling crab who loved to eat seaweed a lot!
Deep down in the ocean was a hungry shark who did not like fish. His favourite thing to eat was crabs.
The hungry shark did not like the beautiful mermaid because he thought she looked scary.
One day, the beautiful mermaid was throwing a huge party for the little crab because he was leaving the sparkling, shiny ocean.
It was time for the crab to leave, so the mermaid's dad and the mermaid were saying goodbye.

Francesca Scholes (7)

Holy Family & St Michael's Catholic Primary School, Pontefract

The Giant Dragon And The Candy Unicorn

A long, long time ago, there was a land called Magical Candy Land. In that land, there was a magical castle called Coloured Candy Castle.

One day, a giant fire-breathing dragon came looking for some food. He couldn't find any! He looked all day but fell asleep.

When he woke up, he heard a noise and blew some fire where he heard the noise.

It was a magical unicorn! The dragon caught the unicorn and tried to drag her away. It was hard to pull her.

She quickly escaped and got away! Before she went, she got her leg and kicked the dragon in the air!

After that, the unicorn went home and lived happily ever after.

Ruby Smith (7)

Holy Family & St Michael's Catholic Primary School, Pontefract

Fantastic Jungle

Once upon a time, I saw scary eyes pointing out of the darkness in the trees. They were huge trees. I could see bushes in front of me.

In the bushes was a snake slithering through the branches. The snake was mad at me. He was sticking his tongue out and he had two sharp teeth. He was really wide. His eyes looked like they were mad at me.

There was a tiger behind a thick tree. He had sharp claws and he had sharp pointed teeth. The tiger was really happy. He ran and jumped over a bush. He ran fast somewhere.

The tiger found a house. He stopped on top of a log. He smiled. He was by two bushes. He was standing silently.

Joshua McLauchlan (7)
Holy Family & St Michael's Catholic Primary School, Pontefract

The Dragon Who Turned Friendly

Once, in a faraway land, there was a castle with an enchanted magical tree. Magicorn was lucky to live in the castle.

One day, a fearsome dragon called Rex flew to the enchanted castle. He was trying to destroy the enchanted castle.

Rex landed on a green hill. He looked very angry. He destroyed the castle with mighty fire. He set the castle on fire.

Magicorn rushed to a very angry Rex. She knew she must stop Rex.

Magicorn used her special powers to turn Rex friendly. Rex flew back to the misty clouds.

Magicorn trotted down the lake, then she had a little rest in a country cottage.

Milena Majcher (6)

Holy Family & St Michael's Catholic Primary School, Pontefract

The Unicorn And The Dragon

Once upon a time, there was a humongous castle.
It looked like a rainbow. It gleamed with beauty.
The trees swayed in the wind.

Then came a frightening dragon, but he was
actually friendly. He had big sharp teeth and sharp
pointy nails.

Then a bigger dragon set the castle on fire! He had
sharp pointy ears and glowing red eyes. He had
purple prickles all over his back.

The kind dragon told him to go away, so he did.

The unicorn fancied the kind dragon.

Then the dragon went away. He said bye and flew
off.

Then the unicorn went home to her rainbow house.

Lucy Marsh (7)
Holy Family & St Michael's Catholic Primary School,
Pontefract

The Dragon Who Turned Friendly

In a faraway land, there was a castle near a magic rainbow. It had lots of colours. Magicorn lived in the castle.

The dangerous dragon flew to the magical land. He was going to destroy Magicorn's castle!

He landed on a tall green hill. He felt mean. He set the castle on fire!

Magicorn rushed to see what was happening. She had to stop him from blowing the castle down.

Magicorn used her secret powers to scare the dragon away through the misty clouds.

She saw a house.

"I think I will stay there for this night."

Julian Rutkowski (6)

Holy Family & St Michael's Catholic Primary School, Pontefract

The Most Exciting Jungle Of All

One day in the deepest, darkest jungle of all, something was peeking out. It looked like eyes. It turned out it was loads of friendly snakes playing hide-and-seek! One snake was the scariest snake and he tried to scare the lions away so they wouldn't get them.

The lion peeked through the long wavy grass to see if he could find the snakes. What he saw scared him, so he ran away from Mr Rattlesnake as fast as his legs could run.

He went back home so he felt safe and calm.

Charlie Gilbert (6)

Holy Family & St Michael's Catholic Primary School, Pontefract

The Spaceship And The Three-Eyed Alien

One day, the rocket was firing into space past a million stars and Mars and the moon. The rocket zoomed past Earth. All of a sudden, the engine began to fail.

A flying saucer came. It had flashing lights. Inside the flying saucer was Mr Moony. He was a kind, happy alien who loved space.

Mr Moony saw the broken rocket and thought, *I should help the rocket*.

Mr Moony and his flying saucer and the rocket went home and he fixed the rocket.

Taylor James Sherburn (6)

Holy Family & St Michael's Catholic Primary School, Pontefract

The Most Exciting Jungle Of All

One day in the darkest jungle of all, something was behind the tree. It was some snakes. It turned out it was lots of thick and strong snakes! They were playing hide-and-seek.

One snake was the scariest snake of all and the snake tried to scare the lions.

A lion went to find the snakes and he went through the grass and he peeked through it. What he saw scared him and he ran away from Mr Rattlesnake. He went home and then he was safe.

Noah Simpson (6)

Holy Family & St Michael's Catholic Primary School, Pontefract

The Most Exciting Jungle Of All

One day in the deepest, darkest jungle of all, something odd was peeking from the dark trees. It turns out it was just a lot of snakes who were playing hide-and-seek!
One snake tried to scare the tigers away because he thought the tiger would eat them.
The tiger went to find the snakes. He peeked through the long swishy grass. What he saw scared him, so he ran away from Mr Rattlesnake! The tiger got home and he felt calm and safe.

Joshua Akrill (5)
Holy Family & St Michael's Catholic Primary School, Pontefract

The Most Exciting Jungle Of All

One day in the deep, dark jungle, something was hiding. You could see the eyes. It turns out it was lots of snakes! They were playing hide-and-seek. One snake tried to scare the lions away so they would not be caught.

One lion went to find the snakes and he went and thought he'd hide in the long wavy grass to find a snake.

What he saw scared him and he ran away from Mr Rattlesnake! He went home and then he was safe.

Harry Vaughan (6)

Holy Family & St Michael's Catholic Primary School, Pontefract

The Spaceship And The Three-Eyed Alien

One day, there was a rocket flying through the stars and past the moon. The rocket flew past the Earth, the land and the sea. All of a sudden, the engine began to fail.

A flying saucer appeared. It had stripes and flashing lights. Inside the spaceship was Mr Moony and Mr Moony loved it in space.

Mr Moony saw the broken rocket and he helped the broken rocket. Mr Moony and the rocket went home and he fixed the rocket.

Tanner Towler (6)

Holy Family & St Michael's Catholic Primary School, Pontefract

The Dragon Who Turned Friendly

In a faraway land, there was a magical castle with a colourful rainbow. Magicorn lived there.
One day, a scary dragon called Rex flew into the magic land. Rex tried to set the castle on fire with an almighty roar.
Magicorn rushed to a very angry Rex. She knew she must stop him. Magicorn used her magic to turn Rex friendly before sending him away.
Magicorn was happy now and she went to her little house to rest.

Filip Truchan (6), Jessica & Pixi-Lil Sands Wright (6)
Holy Family & St Michael's Catholic Primary School, Pontefract

Under The Sea

A boat was on the sparkling ocean. The ocean was getting in the boat.
Under the sea, fishes were swimming in the water. A crab said hi to the fishes.
Suddenly, a shark came and the shark looked terrifying in the sea. But mermaids came and the shark was scared in the deep, dark ocean. The shark was hurt and the mermaids were dancing. The mermaids said goodbye and they lived happily ever after.

Shay Sands Wright (7)

Holy Family & St Michael's Catholic Primary School, Pontefract

The Spaceship And The Three-Eyed Alien

One day, there was a rocket zooming past millions of stars sparkling. The rocket zoomed past Earth and saw the land and the sea. All of a sudden, the engine began to fail.

A flying saucer appeared. It had flashing lights and stripes.

Inside the flying saucer was Mr Moony. He loved it in space!

Mr Moony saw the rocket. He helped the rocket. Mr Moony took the rocket home and fixed the rocket.

Lewis Ward (6)

Holy Family & St Michael's Catholic Primary School, Pontefract

The Mermaid Rescue

Once, there was a boat on the water. It was empty. Under the water was a dancing crab who was having a happy time.

Once under the sea, there was a hungry shark who was called Sharky.

Behind Sharky were Coral and Kingy. Kingy was going to poke Sharky's bum!

Kingy and Coral were dancing when they scared Sharky away! They went back to Mermaid Land.

Angel Loynes (6)

Holy Family & St Michael's Catholic Primary School, Pontefract

The Most Exciting Jungle Of All

One day in the deep, dark jungle, something was hiding. You could see some eyes...
It turned out it was some friendly snakes playing hide-and-seek!
One snake tried to scare some lions away so they would not be caught.
A lion went to look for the snakes, but the scary snake scared him and he ran away. The lion ran all the way home where he was safe.

Riley Parkin (6)
Holy Family & St Michael's Catholic Primary School, Pontefract

The Most Exciting Jungle Of All

One day in the deep, dark jungle, something was hiding. You could see some eyes...

It turned out it was some friendly snakes playing hide-and-seek! One snake tried to scare the lions away so they would not be caught.

One lion wanted to look for the snakes. The snake scared him, so he ran away. The lion ran all the way home where he was safe.

Nathan Addy Sherburn (6)

Holy Family & St Michael's Catholic Primary School, Pontefract

The Spaceship And The Three-Eyed Alien

One day, a rocket shot past the Milky Way. The rocket shot past the Earth. All of a sudden, the engine began to fail.
A spaceship came. It had flashing lights.
Mr Moony was on the moon. Mr Moony saw the broken rocket. He pressed a button. Mr Moony set off to take the rocket home.

Layla Wassel (5)
Holy Family & St Michael's Catholic Primary School, Pontefract

Jack And Alfie Alien

Jack loved everything about aliens and one day he was having an alien birthday party. Jack was sad because he really wanted some real aliens to come to his party, but aliens weren't really real, were they?

His favourite toy he liked to play with was his Alfie the alien teddy. Jack was sure that the Alfie the alien teddy had winked and smiled at him. Jack rubbed his eyes. Was it real, or was he just daydreaming?

Suddenly, Jack sneezed a big massive sneeze and green gooey slime came out of his nose! The green gooey slime melted to create an alien family.

"Hello, Jack, we are the space family. Please to meet you!"

Jack knew that this was going to be the best birthday party he ever had. They danced alien dances, played alien football games and ate alien birthday cake. They even sang alien birthday songs to Jack.

Jack gave the space family aliens a big hug and thanked them for all the fun they had. Alfie smiled and winked at Jack and they could not wait for more alien adventures together.

Ehsaan Asif (6)
Hoyle Court Primary School, Baildon

Emily And Ruby's Magnificent Adventure In The Jungle

One bright sunny morning, Emily and Ruby were playing in the dark, creepy forest which was behind their old dilapidated house. Ruby loved exploring and investigating the world and especially liked solving mysteries and following clues. Emily was quite different. She enjoyed doing sports.

After a while, Ruby found a trail of some dark green leaves, so she shouted: "Emily, I found a trail of some leaves! Let's go explore!"

Emily replied, "But Mum told us to keep safe!"

"Oh, don't be so silly. We're not going to get lost!"

Ruby couldn't wait, so off she went. Emily was extremely nervous because she knew it was dangerous, but she had to keep her sister safe. As soon as they arrived, they found some friends and found out they were in a jungle. They started playing games like: swinging on ropes, dancing games and sport games.

Soon, Emily heard a terrifying sound and screamed, "Come on, everyone, let's explore!"

Ruby loudly said, "It's a tiger, everyone!"

Monkey said, "Go swing on the ropes and we will annoy him by singing loudly."

"Argh! I hate this sound. I'm going to go back," said Emily.

Ruby mumbled, "I think that's our mum. Goodbye!"

The animals were upset to see Emily and Ruby go, but they were going to remember the fun they had together and said, "You can come here whenever you want to, Emily and Ruby."

Emily and Ruby replied, "We will try to come back one day, we promise! We will remember the fun we had forever and ever."

Hirah Mahmood (7)

IQRA Academy, Manningham

The Fierce Dragon And The Magical Unicorns

Once upon a time, there was an enormous, beautiful castle which was next to a tall tree with a colourful rainbow.

Suddenly, a fierce fire-breathing dragon came to attack the castle because he didn't like the colour of it. People in the castle were scared because the dragon was attacking them. This news spread as quick as wildfire. People started to write it in newspapers.

The dragon's wings were as big as a giant elephant's ears. Whenever the dragon breathed fire, it could burn and destroy things.

People tried to kill the fierce dragon, but they couldn't. Most people thought they would have died, but some said, "We're going to beat him up!" Everyone tried to attack him, but they couldn't. Suddenly, two unicorns came and used their magic by taking all the dragon's strength. Now the dragon was so weak and the unicorns were so strong. They had a fight again and something amazing happened! The unicorns won because they defeated the dragon!

All the people in the castle were filled with happiness because they won! The castle had broken down, so they said, "Let's rebuild the castle!"

This time, they were going to put a padlock on. If someone wanted to destroy the castle, they would have to have a password! But if someone nice wanted to come in and they knew the password, they could cross the path.

Everyone lived happily ever after and nothing happened again.

Ahmed Mohamed Khaled Eldaly (7)

IQRA Academy, Manningham

Exploring Giant Planets Of Space

It was a quiet, dark night when a small boy called Tom and a small, friendly girl called Sarah found themselves awake. They couldn't sleep because they were excited to explore space just like Yuri Gagarin did in 1961. They loved space and they loved twinkling stars.

After a while, they slowly tiptoed into their kind parents' giant room and quietly whispered to their dad, "Can we go to space?"

Dad replied, "Only if you promise not to get into trouble."

"We won't," they said.

Now they were filled with excitement, so they quietly opened the old grey garage and got out their rusty old giant UFO.

A few minutes later, when they had finally put the black fuel in, they zoomed off like a shooting star. While they were looking around this marvellous place, they spied a planet they'd never seen before.

Sarah asked, "Could that be Pluto?"

Tom replied, "It is Pluto!"

Millions of aliens were dancing with joy and eating scrumptious food. It was a disco! Tom and Sarah were so jolly that they joined in too.

The slimy green aliens said, "Welcome!" and let them have mouthwatering pizza.

Soon it was starting to get lighter, so Sarah and Tom set off home happily with their amazing story. At first, Mum didn't believe their story, but when Dad told her it was true, she said, "Alright, I believe you."

Talha Ali Khan (7)
IQRA Academy, Manningham

Fun Adventures Under The Blue Sea

Once upon a time, there lived two lovely girls named Rosey and Lola. One day, the two girls went to school and learnt about the sea. That day, they were so busy thinking about the ocean.
After a couple of months, they went on holiday to the beach.
Their mum said, "Follow me!"
They tiptoed and followed her as quiet as mice. A few minutes later, they went the wrong way in the deep blue sea! They saw some fish and stroked them very carefully.
Then Rosie spotted a dangerous shark coming towards them! Lola got a stick and they tried to push the shark away. The shark felt the stick, so he got really angry. He swam away, leaving white popping bubbles behind him.
The fish were so happy that they didn't get eaten. The fish said, "Would you two like to have a jolly party?"
The two girls replied, "Yes!"
So they all had a nice time. They danced and had yummy cake.

The shark could hear the wonderful music, so he started dancing with his dangerous friends.

Their mum saw the girls in the ocean. They saw her, so they said goodbye to their new friends and swam towards her. They climbed out and told their amazing mum what happened. She was shocked that a shark had come next to them.

The shark never came back again. The fish were happy that they didn't get eaten by sharks.

Maryam Patel (6)

IQRA Academy, Manningham

The Jungle Animals

In a deep forest, there lived a long, angry snake and a fluffy, cute, small lion. The snake was happily slithering along the muddy and grassy floor. He was slithering for so long that he got tired and he had a rest.

Suddenly, the snake smelt something. He thought he could eat it, so he hissed so loud that the fluffy and cute lion could hear him. The fast and furry lion got really scared. The problem was that the snake wasn't friends with anyone because the snake was mean.

The lion had a plan, but he had to find the snake before he could do it. He found the snake slithering to his favourite tree stump. The lion ran as fast as he could. Finally, he got to the snake. The snake turned around and saw the lion.

The lion said, "If you don't be kind to others, they won't be kind to you."

Misbah Inayah Ali (7)
IQRA Academy, Manningham

The Dinosaur Story

Once upon a time, there lived a girl called Lilly. One day, she woke up and looked outside. She saw a black machine, so she ran downstairs to check it out. Then she climbed in and it took her to Dinosaur Land!

Lilly opened her eyes slowly and there were dinosaurs walking everywhere. There was a T-rex walking towards Lilly. She didn't know what to do, so she said, "Stop!"

The T-rex stopped and leaned over and there were three white eggs. Lilly remembered a book she was reading. It was about how T-rexes looked after their children. The T-rex roared to stop the other dinosaurs trying to get the three white eggs.

Eiliyah Aftab (7)

IQRA Academy, Manningham

Under The Sea

Once upon a time, there was a blue, deep sea. Under the sea, there was a handsome king called King Bob and his daughter called Mermaid Ariel. They had a boat in the middle of the sea. The sea was very clear and wavy. The sea had colourful coral. Under the sea, there were beautiful animals. Out of the middle of nowhere, a shark came! The shark was trying to be friendly, but they didn't listen and they terrified the shark away because they thought he would hurt them.

After that, the king and the mermaid invited all the fishes to a party.

Ali Irfan (7)

IQRA Academy, Manningham

Under The Sea

A long, long time ago in the light blue sea, there was a boat on the wobbly sea. Under the boat lived sea creatures and a mermaid and a king, and the sea creatures loved to swim. They swam forever and never stopped.

The mermaid and king were at home. The boats were up there alone.

Suddenly, a shark came to play with someone, but the mermaid and king came with a big fork and scared him away, because they thought he was gonna eat the sea creatures. The king and mermaid invited everyone and had a party and swam away happily.

Sudais Khan (7)
IQRA Academy, Manningham

The Crab And The Mermaids

There was a boat. It was wooden and it was left there on its own. It just stood there. It was boring. It was brown and no one saw the boat. It seriously stood there... for no reason...

Then a happy crab came by! It was playing! There were lots of pebbles and rocks. There were also lots of seashells. There were millions of fish and crabs!

Then a scary shark came by to eat the crab! The crab ran... and ran... and ran home. The shark laughed and laughed and swam towards the mermaid's house.

Until... the mermaid chased off the shark! The shark was chased off! The shark was terrified, so the shark ran home!

The crab was saved! They were all happy. And they danced... so they wanted to be the crab's friend! They asked the crab.

They saw a boat and put it on an island. Someone found the missing boat and the mermaids were happy! They went home...

Iva Drevina (7)
New Bewerley Community School, Beeston

The Happy Underwater

Once, there was a mysterious boat in a big sea. It floated away. No one knew who it belonged to. Deep underground, there was a crab. It was a big crab, not a small crab. It was very strong.

One day, a shark was searching for some food. It was always hungry, but now it was *very* hungry! Then a mermaid came and scared it away. That day, he would not come out again. He promised they would never see him again.

Then the mermaid announced that that was what she wanted. She danced!

Finally, she saw the boat.

The king said, "I've found my boat now! Look at my beautiful boat, it looks brand new!"

You should know something: they are always happy.

Jainaba Drammeh (7)
New Bewerley Community School, Beeston

The Little Mermaid

Once upon a time, there was a boat and it was just staying still in the water. There was nobody around it.

In the sea, there were some little fish and there was also a little crab and the crab was really happy.

Then there was a shark in the water and the shark was trying to get the little mermaid. Then the shark saw the little mermaid and the shark didn't know what to do! Then her father came. When her father came, her father scared the shark away and the little mermaid was safe.

The little shark went away to his little home and then the little mermaid lived happily ever after.

Honey Allotey (7)
New Bewerley Community School, Beeston

The Secret Under The Sea

One day, there was a secret boat. No one knew whose it was except the shark. It started drifting off and a crab got fascinated by it. He kept looking at the bottom of the boat.

Suddenly, a shark came! But the crab hid too quickly. The shark stayed around. He didn't leave, he didn't give up.

Then a mermaid came and shouted, "I'll use my magic to push you into the deep pool of horror if you don't tell us whose the boat is!"

The shark said it was his and ran off.

Everybody was so happy that they had a party and then went up to see the boat.

Anisa Quereshi (7)

New Bewerley Community School, Beeston

The Ocean

There was a boat that was alone. It was there for a year, but nobody knew.
The crab didn't see the boat, so he looked around the sea. He was thinking about something.
A shark was going to get the crab for his dinner, so he sped up to get the crab!
The mermaid was gonna get eaten by the shark, but a brave man was coming! It was Merman and he saved the mermaid.
They had a party, so the crab joined and a seafish. They had a great time!
They waved at the crab and they went into the sea.

Ismael Rahim (7)
New Bewerley Community School, Beeston

The World Of Mermaids

Once, there was an old, grey, mysterious boat on top of a silent ocean.

Under the boat was a little red crab and some little colourful, beautiful, happy fish.

But then a nasty shark came. The shark wanted to eat the happy fish and the crab.

Suddenly, a mermaid came and chased the shark away. Then a mermaid came along and helped.

Then the mermaid and the merman had a party. The crab came and even a seahorse!

Then it was time to go home and the merman and mermaid waved bye-bye.

Lily-Mai Simpson (7)
New Bewerley Community School, Beeston

Under The Sea

First, there was a mysterious boat and at the bottom of the boat there was a mysterious mermaid and a merman.

There was a crab as well and the crab went to the surface to see what that mysterious boat was doing.

The crab saw what was coming, so he turned around and went in his shell so a passing shark couldn't get him.

Then the merman tried to kill the shark, so the shark swam away!

The merman and mermaid had a party and the crab floated away in the boat.

Louie Naylor (7)
New Bewerley Community School, Beeston

The Boat And The Mermaid

Once, there was a boat. No one was in that boat.
A crab saw the boat on top of the sea, but everyone else saw something different...
It was a shark! Every fish and crab hid super quick, but someone was running over...
It was the mermaid! The mermaid then shooed the shark away from getting the fish.
Then they all had a party and everyone shouted, "Hooray!"
Then the mermaid checked out what everyone had been looking at. It was the boat!

Nickolas Lupu (7)
New Bewerley Community School, Beeston

The Magic Princess

One sunny day, a princess was sleeping in a castle and then she heard a stomping noise. She looked out of her window and saw a dragon!
The dragon blew and blew until the dragon saw a unicorn.
The unicorn met up with the dragon. She said, "You're the best."
"Oh my," said the dragon.
"Come over to my house."
"Sorry, I can't."
"But I will come to your house!" the princess shouted.
"No, don't, you will be dead!"
"Sorry, sorry," said the princess.
"You better be sorry!" said the dragon.

Freya Ann Winterbottom (6)
Oulton Primary School, Oulton

Under The Sea

Once upon a time, there lived a lady called Jam who travelled on a boat to London. She lived in Asia and had learnt to speak English.
She saw a snappy crab and fish and smelly squid.
"Oh no! A shark is here, what should I do next?"
She tried to stop him. He didn't stop.
Her dad was trying to talk to her and the shark swam away because of the shouting.
They danced! Then they got moving again.

Lexi Rae Bruce (6)
Oulton Primary School, Oulton

Boat Adventure

Once upon a time, someone called Fin was sailing. He wanted to go for a long dive, but when he went for a dive he suddenly turned into an amazing mermaid!

Then he saw another amazing mermaid being chased by a shark! The magical mermaid went to save the other mermaid without being gobbled up! Then he said, "Shoo!" and the shark swam away. Finally, they wanted to stay and they celebrated.

Oscar Filip Shirripa (6)
Oulton Primary School, Oulton

The Story Dragon

Once upon a time, there was a machine and it made dinosaurs.

One day, all the dinosaurs were all alone because the machine was not working.

Then a dragon spotted some eggs, so the dragon went to the eggs. The dragon took one.

Then a dinosaur came and the dinosaur said, "Where is my missing egg? Someone has got it."

But then the machine was working again, so everyone was happy!

Alana-Rose Rawson (6)
Oulton Primary School, Oulton

Lily And Magic

The fairy lived in a castle and she was nice. Her name was Lily.
The dragon wasn't nice to the fairy and he blew fire. The dragon was trying to scare Lily the fairy. But... a beautiful unicorn called Magic came to save Lily the fairy from the dragon!
Magic scared the naughty dragon away and saved Lily the fairy. Lily and Magic lived in Lily's palace happily ever after.

Lily P (6)
Oulton Primary School, Oulton

The Magical Unicorn

Once upon a time, there lived a princess called Isabella and Rose the unicorn. Rose was rainbow coloured and she lived in a castle with a different-coloured rainbow over the top. She was always friendly. Rose had magical powers to control things. Isabella had a beautiful palace to live in, but the unicorn didn't live in the castle.

But while Rose was eating green grass, a dragon called Jeff crept up on Rose and tried to attack her. He wasn't nice to other things. When Jeff was trying to attack Rose, she suddenly disappeared, then he lost her. When she tried to run, she returned to her normal colour and Jeff saw her. Jeff tried to breathe very, very hot fire at Rose, but he missed her. The dragon was getting angry because he missed her again.

Then Rose pretended to be kind to Jeff, but she actually hurt him on one of his paws.

Jeff flew back to where he lived far, far away. That was the end of the dragon. He went home and never came back.

Then Rose had a very nice sleep.

Paige Hope Ross (7)

Ravenfield Primary Academy, Ravenfield

My Fantastic Day Under The Water

One *mermazing* day, I felt like having a mermaid adventure, so I jumped into my boat and sailed away. I trailed my hand in the water and it felt enchanting. As soon as I could, I dived in.

While I was underwater, I saw a crab. His name was Sebastian and he was looking for a new shell. Then he said, "There are so many wonders in the sea, but there is a shark that won't let you look at his treasure."

Suddenly, without knowing, Sebastian took me to the shark's cave. At first I didn't see anything, but as soon as I looked away I saw a glance of a mermaid trying to steal the shark's treasure.

With nothing to do, I swam into the cave and saw the mermaid. I was amazed. To help the mermaid, I snatched the treasure off the shark and swam for the mermaid's coral.

When we arrived at the mermaid's coral, her father was amazed at how she got the treasure. I stayed for tea and we talked about how we got the treasure.

They swam up to the surface with me and, from that day on, I could come over whenever I wanted. The next time I went, they had two baddies called Oceana and Mermaida...

Emily Woodcock (7)

Ravenfield Primary Academy, Ravenfield

The King Snake

One sunny morning in the jungle, some eyes were in the trees' darkness. The leaves were as green as emeralds. The branches were as brown as an owl. Alfie the snake came to a world of snakes and one other animal who he did not know. Every snake in the forest did not like him, but Alfie thought the other animal in the forest might like him.

One day, Alfie met the king of the snakes. The king wanted to kill every animal in the forest except himself. Alfie was shocked and Alfie slithered away until he was tired. All the other snakes slithered with him.

Alfie bumped into the creature who he did not know. It was a lion called James! All the other snakes did not see him because they went in a different direction.

James said, "I have heard about the news."

James ran through the trees to get to the king's house. Alfie was slithering to get help.

Alfie got to the other snakes and said, "We need to get to the king's house, we will meet a friendly lion."

Finally, James got to the king's house and met Alfie and the other snakes. They stole the king's jewellery.

Beau Lawton (6)

Ravenfield Primary Academy, Ravenfield

The Magical Unicorn

One magical day, there was a castle that could take you to the future. The castle had some beautiful unicorns inside. The unicorns flew around. But one of the unicorns had disappeared and it was the baby unicorn!

But they found her. She was on top of the roof. Then she went off again! This time she was actually lost. She had been found by the terrifying dragon...

The terrible dragon breathed fire. It had found the other sparkly rainbow unicorn. Just at that moment, the unicorns introduced themselves.

"I'm called Sparkle, my daughter is called Precious."

Afterwards, the unicorns let the dragon have a look around their sparkly castle. Then they let the dragon have dinner.

After dinner, the dragon said goodbye. The unicorns waved goodbye and put some shiny stars in the sky.

The unicorns kept writing letters to the dragon and the dragon wrote letters back to them. From then on, they were best friends. Each time the dragon came, the unicorns knew.

Isabell Davis (6)

Ravenfield Primary Academy, Ravenfield

The Magical Unicorn And The Horrifying Dragon

Once upon a time, there lived a mythical unicorn. She was colourful. Then she saw a beautiful blue and white castle with a colourful rainbow over the top of it.

But then a gigantic dark green dragon landed next to the castle. He had claws as sharp as daggers, wings as large as houses and ears as pointy as mountains.

But the dragon was going to breathe fire on the beautiful blue and white castle! He was about to when the unicorn began to gallop to him.

Then when she went to him, she pretended she loved the ugly, mean old fellow and put her beautiful silver hoof into his ugly gleen claws. The unicorn smiled at him. The dragon smiled back.

Then the unicorn pretended she was going to kiss him, but then she stabbed him with her beautiful silver horn.

The dragon leapt everywhere and flew away. The unicorn was delighted! Then the unicorn found a house and lay down next to it with the moonlight and stars shining above her.

Katie Wood (7)
Ravenfield Primary Academy, Ravenfield

Tom The Spaceman

Once upon a time, there was a boy called Tom. Tom was bored, so he got into his rocket and he flew far away from Earth.

He heard a sound because the alert button was beeping and he had to fix it. He landed on the moon. He had to fix the engine. The alert button stopped beeping and it went quiet in the rocket. The rocket was missing something and Tom had to fix it.

Suddenly, a spaceship landed on the moon and Tom was surprised. It was a spaceship with an alien inside. Tom was scared because he thought it was a mean alien but it wasn't. It was a friendly alien and the alien waved at Tom. Tom waved back at him and suddenly they became friends together.

The alien beamed Tom and his space rocket up and the alien waved again and Tom waved back at him. Tom smiled at the alien. The alien smiled back at him.

The alien took Tom home and he was happy about his adventures that day.

"Thank you," said Tom.

They were happy together because they had fun.

Theo Priestley (7)
Ravenfield Primary Academy, Ravenfield

114

The Jungle

One dull, dark day, there was a lonely young snake called Bob. He lived in an old forest that was haunted. Every day, he explored the old forest. Bob went into the forest one day and found a big bad snake. He didn't know that he wasn't friendly... Suddenly, he was caught by the unfriendly snake. He didn't shut his eyes and got hypnotised, then fell into a deep sleep with his eyes open.

Luckily, a tiger came to his rescue and really hurt the snake. He scratched his claw straight down his back. He had blood dripping down his back.

Tiger said, "Bob, do you know your way around the jungle?"

"Yes," said the lion.

"Can you take me home?"

Just then, he got caught by the snake again! Tiger flung him around.

After, Tiger stood on a log and looked for the snake's house. Afterwards, he found Snake's home. Then they waved goodbye and saw each other every day.

James Wood (7)

Ravenfield Primary Academy, Ravenfield

The Jungle

One fresh morning in the mysterious jungle, when you looked at the leaves they were as green as you could ever imagine and the branches were as brown as fresh wood. Some of the animals that lived in it were the scaly snakes. The kindest snake in the jungle was Jeffrey and he wouldn't hurt anyone.

One day, the king snake declared in a meeting that he would kill all the animals in the jungle, including all of the snakes apart from himself, because he wanted to be the last animal standing in the jungle. All of the other snakes got furious and hissed at the king.

Jeffrey went to cuddly Tim the lion to tell him all about what the king had said. Tim could not believe what he was hearing. Jeffrey and Tim went to get help. Tim went left and Jeffrey went right. But guess what? Tim didn't realise he had made a big mistake and had gone in the direction of the king's house! He was never heard from again...

Bobby Parkin (7)
Ravenfield Primary Academy, Ravenfield

The Magical Unicorn And The Dreadful Dragon

Once upon a magical world, there was a magical castle owned by a magical unicorn named Lyla. She loved it in her magical world because there was a rainbow waterfall. There also were a couple of dragons on that world. Each morning, Lyla leapt out of bed hearing dreadful noises and roars.

One night, the dragon's father could hear Lyla singing in the castle. He got so fed up with it and got so mad that he tried to set the castle on fire! He forgot all about the waterfall and it luckily put out the fire.

Lyla came galloping out. She galloped into the dragon's son. She made a deal with him that they would scare each other. When it was Lyla's turn, she actually scared the dragon! He flew off like lightning. After, she ran home.

Finally, she was home. She went in, got in her bath, stayed in for a couple of refreshing hours and then got in her pyjamas and went to bed.

Alexia Wild (7)
Ravenfield Primary Academy, Ravenfield

The Magical Unicorn And The Horrifying Dragon

Once upon a time, there was a pretty princess called Poppy. She was a very nice princess. She helped lots and lots of people, but her father didn't like her so she was kept in her castle.

Suddenly, there was a dragon. He was very nasty and didn't like anyone. He came upon the castle where the princess lived.

Then the dragon was breathing fire at Poppy! Poppy was terrified and she was shaking. The castle was almost burnt down! The dragon looked very scary because it had scales on its back and fire like a volcano.

Suddenly, a unicorn came along and Poppy was shocked. Then the unicorn used its powers on the dragon.

The unicorn had sparkles around her and then the dragon stopped breathing fire at the castle. Then the unicorn made it go away. Then the unicorn went home and the princess was fine. From then on, the unicorn saved the princess from any danger.

Rubi Zahir (7)

Ravenfield Primary Academy, Ravenfield

The King Cobra

Once upon a jungle, there lived many animals. At night, all you could see were many snowy white eyes that looked blankly at each other. Then in the morning, you could see the snakes themselves, slithering around the jungle floor. One day, the Snake King's son came.

This wicked king said he hated his son because he lived happily with the snakes and helped them. The king was jealous. He declared that he would kill every single snake that lived in the jungle. But the day he tried to kill them, proud, kind Lion approached! He was the strongest creature in the jungle. No one could defeat him. He saw the snakes were in danger, so he crept up to the king and chased him away.

The king was never seen again. The lion was made king. As for the snakes, they were turned into his servants and guards, which they loved.

The lion left the jungle and was given a palace of his own.

Rohan Gray (7)
Ravenfield Primary Academy, Ravenfield

Terror In Time

One dinorific afternoon, I was watching TV when I saw my name. It was Professor Nimbus, so I grabbed my binoculars and made a packed lunch, then I went to the professor and went back in time. I saw dinosaurs galore! I had my lunch on a raptor's back and made a new friend.

Suddenly, my delicious lunch was interrupted by a group of dinosaurs. Seven T-rexes started to run at me. My raptor ran for his life with me clutching onto his back!

Then, from the corner of my eye, I saw the T-rexes weren't running for me, they were running for some eggs! My raptor jumped to get them, but was too late...

Then I noticed a pterodactyl above us. I threw a rope and it caught it. I swung and grabbed the eggs and gave them to the mum.

I jumped on a seat, set the machine to 'present' and said bye to my prehistoric friends.

Reece Ramskill (7)

Ravenfield Primary Academy, Ravenfield

A Mermazing Under The Water Day

One mermazing day, I went to the sea. As soon as I dipped my foot in the water, my amulet glowed and I turned into a mermaid. When I slid down into the water, I realised I could breathe under the water. There were so many nice creatures, like a red crab called Sebastian and a fish called Flounder. Suddenly, a bad shark came. It wasn't any old shark, it was Ursula's shark! The shark smiled. When he smiled, you could see his sharp white teeth. Just at that moment, King Triton got out his trident and pointed it at the shark to save me.

King Triton and I were best friends. We were dancing and singing all night. We never wanted to leave each other, so we married.

Because the king was a merking, I turned into a merqueen and we had two merbabies called Coral Pearl and Oceana Shell.

Summer Rose Muffett (6)

Ravenfield Primary Academy, Ravenfield

The Magical World

Once upon a time, there lived a princess called Olivia. Olivia lived in a castle with a Unicorn called Glitter. She was scared to leave the castle because of an evil dragon called Clumsy. Do you know why he was called Clumsy? Because he made spells which went wrong and dropped things.

One day, Clumsy was looking through the window for Princess Olivia, he was puffing smoking fire. Then Glitter opened the gate to the castle and said, "Follow me, Clumsy." Clumsy followed Glitter to the garden.

Then Clumsy sat down next to Glitter. Glitter was kind and said, "Please be kind to Princess Olivia and stop trying to put a spell on her."

The dragon flew off and went back to his village!

From then on, Princess Olivia and Glitter lived happily ever after.

Darcey Beth Allsop (7)

Ravenfield Primary Academy, Ravenfield

A Visit To Seaquestria

One mermazing day, I went fishing on a rowing boat. Then I saw something shiny in the water. I dived in, then I realised I had a mermaid tail!

I saw a crab called Sebastian and a fish called Flounder. I saw a whole underwater castle and Flounder was so cute and cuddly.

Then a shark was swimming towards me with its jaws snapping. I swam as fast as I could, then, when I looked behind me, the shark was gone. Then the shark sprang out and grabbed me!

Then the king mermaid grabbed his magic staff and charged at the shark. Then the shark spotted him and swam away.

I said, "Thank you!" then me and the king did a little victory dance.

After that, it was time I went home. From then on when I went fishing, I would dive down to Seaquestria.

Sophie Needle (7)
Ravenfield Primary Academy, Ravenfield

The Enchanted Castle

One glorious day, there was a castle that wasn't an ordinary castle - it was a magical castle! Outside, it felt enchanting.

Outside lived a strong, muscular and tough dragon. He had large wings and razor-sharp claws. The fierce dragon roared and fire rushed out of his mouth. As I started fighting, he quickly pushed me over. Without hesitation, I stood up.

Suddenly, in the corner of my eye, a magical unicorn appeared at the side of me. The dragon made friends with the unicorn.

Afterwards, the dragon flew away in the sky and the magical unicorn waved goodbye. As the dragon left, the unicorn sprinkled some magical dust on him. From then on, they were best friends. The unicorn never forgot the dragon.

Eden Grace Ross (7)
Ravenfield Primary Academy, Ravenfield

An Amazing Jungle Adventure

Once upon a jungle, I woke up and looked around. I was in a jungle. I couldn't believe my eyes. I was amazed. I saw a snake slithering by. I was very, very *confused.com*. I was looking for food. I was starving, so I looked to the right and looked to the left, but saw nothing.

A king cobra was slithering by. I was very, very, very scared. But it was not an ordinary snake, it was king of the jungle and he wanted to kill all of the other snakes.

Lion overheard this and started to run and run and run on his way to the snakes. The lion told the snakes what he heard. The snakes were horrified. So he just went back. From then on, he was the best lion in the world and everyone agreed.

Charlotte Mary Sanderson (6)
Ravenfield Primary Academy, Ravenfield

Long Before Time

One dinorific afternoon, I was watching TV and I saw a time machine. Then I went to the shop and bought it.

Suddenly, I found myself next to a stegosaurus and an apatosaurus and they were friendly.

Suddenly, I was interrupted by a ferocious roar. I recognised it as a T-rex! I saw it was going to get something in the leaves...

I realised it was a group of eggs! I knew they were pterodactyl eggs, so I made a distraction. I said, "Come and get me!"

Then I heard a squawk. It was the mummy pterodactyl and she swooped the eggs up and took them home.

But I was still running from the T-rex! In the bushes, I saw the time machine, then I went back home.

Archie Ridley (7)
Ravenfield Primary Academy, Ravenfield

Dinosaur Day!

James was playing at the park. He found a time machine. James pressed a button and went back in time.

There were dinosaurs everywhere! He was so excited. He had never met a dinosaur before. He made friends with a dinosaur called Sophie. Sophie took him for a walk. James had a piggyback from Sophie. They played for hours. James came across dinosaur eggs. Suddenly, one hatched in front of him. James named the dinosaur baby Reece.

James looked up as Reece started flying. Sophie took James to a park.

The time machine was on the floor. James knew it time to go home. He missed his mummy and daddy. But James did have a fun day.

James Wharin (7)
Ravenfield Primary Academy, Ravenfield

Cruz In A Rocket

Once upon a time, there was a little boy. Cruz went to his grandad and said, "Grandad, can you build a rocket ship for me?"

"Yes, I can!"

Cruz played in it all the time!

Two days ago, Cruz saw a big red button and it was a boost! He launched off into space!

"Help, help!"

He saw a little light and it got bigger and bigger and bigger. It was a spaceship! The door opened and he saw an alien.

"Help, it's an alien!"

But the alien smiled and they were friends.

The alien lifted up Cruz and his space rocket and took them home. Cruz never flew the rocket again.

Cruz Lee Pearce (7)
Ravenfield Primary Academy, Ravenfield

The Magic Castle

One sunny morning, there was a princess called Poppy. She was very kind.

When the dragon arrived, he found the princess in the throne room. The dragon got hold of her in his claws and then the dragon got her and took her to his lair, but he dropped her. She ran away, thinking she would be safe.

One night, the dragon came back. He breathed fire into all the rooms and they got burnt down. The princess was safe.

The unicorn used magic on the dragon and made him into a nice dragon. The dragon went to his lair. From then on, the princess always told the unicorn if she was in danger.

Sophia Lucy Wagstaff (6)
Ravenfield Primary Academy, Ravenfield

The Alien And The Boy

One day, I put on my oxygen tank and my helmet and I boarded my ship, but my engine overheated. A lot of smoke came out. My heart beat very fast like a roller coaster. When I landed, my ship's wing came off.

Then I saw a light, bigger, bigger and bigger. A spaceship landed and the door opened. I looked inside...

Then I looked down and saw Three-Eye. I ran behind a moon rock. Suddenly, the alien was waving at me!

The alien could not fix my ship because he had no tools. The alien beamed me up from the planet. When we got home, the alien fixed my rocket and waved goodbye.

Oliver Patrick Wild (7)

Ravenfield Primary Academy, Ravenfield

The Jungle

One misty day in a jungle, there lived a king cobra called Max and a tiger called Bob.

Bob was sunbathing, but Max was starting to get very mad and Bob was getting very scared and ran away.

But Max was faster than Bob, so he caught up with him and Bob hid in the bush. Max gave up and Bob was more than happy.

Bob started to get happier and happier and happier. Max was definitely not happy, so he got annoyed.

Bob started to head back home and he ran and ran and ran until he got back home.

When Bob got home, it was his bedtime.

Charlie Hobson (7)
Ravenfield Primary Academy, Ravenfield

The Magic Castle And The Unicorn

Once, there was a mythical castle that had a unicorn and a princess living together inside it. The unicorn belonged to the princess.

One damp, dark night, a dragon appeared and the dragon tried to destroy the castle! The dragon set everything on fire and the castle and the village started to burn down.

The unicorn came to save the day and the unicorn used some of her magic and the dragon was so scared. He was so scared that he flew away, even though he wanted to stay.

The unicorn was so happy that she'd saved the day.

Sadie Wharton (7)

Ravenfield Primary Academy, Ravenfield

Once Upon A Time

Once upon a time, there was a boy called Bob and he was exploring the woods and it was nine o'clock. He saw little eyes and he accidentally stepped on a snake and the snake tried to kill him! The snake got angry, it was a rattlesnake. Bob ran and ran and ran.

But something came... it was a tiger! But it wasn't an ordinary tiger, it was a very strong tiger and he went back home. He saw some meat and when he saw his house he said, "I can see my house!"

He got on his log and saw his house.

Ben Saville (7)
Ravenfield Primary Academy, Ravenfield

The Land Before Time

Once upon a time, I looked in my shed and found a time portal. I turned it to 'past'.

I was in the dinosaur land! I saw a dinosaur who was eating leaves with a baby dinosaur.

Suddenly, a T-rex appeared and scared me. The T-rex found some eggs and was going for the eggs! But Mrs Pterodactyl got the eggs and gave them back to the dinosaur who owned them.

Then I ran back to the time portal and was back at my house.

Harry Thewlis (7)
Ravenfield Primary Academy, Ravenfield

Are Aliens Real?

Once upon a time, a boy called Tim got in his rocket and blasted off to space.
His rocket broke on the moon. Tim was stuck on the moon.
An alien spaceship came by. An alien waved at Tim.
Tim said, "I need help with my rocket."
The alien beamed the rocket up and got Tim inside the spaceship. The alien took him and his rocket home.

Alfie Whitehouse (7)

Ravenfield Primary Academy, Ravenfield

The Faraway Land

The magic chair began to glow and took me into the past. We went through a machine that could take you into a magical land. It mostly never worked, but this time it did.

We landed in a land full of scary dinosaurs. We found out that they were the friendly dinosaurs. I always wondered what they were.

But then we saw a really fierce dinosaur, but I knew about it because my dinosaur friends told me about it.

Then we saw the dinosaurs' eggs and one of them looked like it was going to hatch. I was petrified because I wasn't sure whether it was going to be a nice dinosaur like the others.

Guess what? It hatched to be a friendly one and it flew us back to the magic chair. I was scared, sad and pleased because I was leaving my friends, it felt like I was going to drop and I was leaving nasty dinosaurs, just going home.

Yay! We were back home. I was shattered and very pleased to be back home. I ran up the garden path to go home and enjoy myself. I kept this adventure a secret.

Lucy Anne Rose (7)
Southroyd Primary School, Pudsey

Danger In The Sea

One day, I was sailing on my beautiful wooden boat. Suddenly, something bumped into my boat and I fell off into the astonishing ocean!
As I fell deeper and deeper, I saw crabs and fish playing happily, but in the distance I saw a terrifying shark coming to me and the fish...
A few seconds later, I warned the turtles, crabs and fish. They scurried to their homes. The shark was trying to eat anything!
The shark seemed scary, but was a scaredy-cat. I saw a mermaid coming to save us. She tried as hard as she could. The shark swam away, terrified. Did it work...?
Yes, it did! How could that have happened? She'd saved the day! Everyone couldn't believe their own eyes. Everyone was cheering as loud as they could. Then the merman and the mermaid swam to my boat and I said thank you and sailed away...

Aimee Rose Hunt (7)
Southroyd Primary School, Pudsey

The Unicorn And The Dragon

One day, there was a beautiful castle and the flags meant people were in. The amazing rainbow came out instead of the rain.

The next day, a hideous dragon appeared. The dragon was also nasty. The dragon made a plan to destroy the castle. The dragon breathed fire to knock down the castle. He destroyed it a little bit. Then a unicorn arrived! The unicorn was stronger than the dragon, so the unicorn could beat the dragon up.

The dragon left at last. The dragon went to his home. The unicorn was so happy that the dragon went home.

The unicorn went home as well. Not seeing dragons anymore!

Mia Hemingway (7)
Southroyd Primary School, Pudsey

A Jungle Snake

One day in a jungle, I saw something very scary. In-between trees were thousands of eyes watching me.

Suddenly, a snake came to rescue me. It was very nice. I held its tail. The snake turned back on me. It looked as if it was gonna eat me!

A lion came and scared the snake. It was very nice. I liked the lion.

After that, I played tig with the lion and hide-and-seek. The lion liked playing with me, but it was then time to go.

Finally, I got ready to go home. I said, "See you next time I come to play!"

Pippa-Rose Keough (5)

Southroyd Primary School, Pudsey

The Magic Unicorn

Once upon a time, there was a beautiful, magical and sparkling castle. In the castle, there was a red and scary dragon.

Then the dragon breathed fire out of his mouth and he spat it onto the beautiful, magical castle. Suddenly, the dragon saw a magic unicorn! She said, "What have you done to my magic castle?" After that, the magic unicorn cast a spell on the dragon and the dragon flew away.

Then the unicorn found a house and she hopped to the house, then she was happy.

Harleen Panesar (6)
Southroyd Primary School, Pudsey

Toby's Space Story

Once upon a time, there was a rocket in space. I didn't know where it was going.

It went around the world. Everyone was speechless and shocked.

Then we saw a weird aircraft flying around in space.

"Oh, I know what it is. It's a spaceship."

Then an alien appeared! He said, "My name is Jack."

The cute little alien lifted the rocket up, but why?

The rocket landed near a base. There was a kid in the rocket! It was his home.

Toby James Grayson (7)
Southroyd Primary School, Pudsey

Under The Sea

A little wooden boat was in the cold water. Why was no one controlling it?
A big smiling crab was waving to his friends. There were all kinds of fish.
Suddenly, a big shark came! His teeth were sharp as razors.
Suddenly, the king came with his daughter and chased the scary shark away.
The sea creatures and the king and his daughter had a party. The king and his daughter had a little dance by the wooden boat. They lived happily ever after.

Adam Tasker (6)
Southroyd Primary School, Pudsey

Unicorns And Dragons

Once upon a time, there was a palace in the middle of the town. One day, there was an evil dragon and he was coming to set it on fire! After a few minutes, the mad dragon went and blew fire at the castle window. Then came a unicorn with her magic horn and the dragon got scared and tried to stop her! But he could not, so he flew away and disappeared into the clouds.

After that, it was night-time. The unicorn went inside to sleep all night.

Autumn Isabelle McDonald (6)

Southroyd Primary School, Pudsey

Jaden's Space Story

Once upon a time, there was a rocket. People in the rocket saw a football pitch. Some robbers were taking a football trophy. The people in the rocket went down to Earth. There was a big, big fight. The people saved the trophy for the World Cup. Everyone cheered!
Then the alien popped back into the rocket!
Then everything went back to normal.

Jaden Thiara (6)
Southroyd Primary School, Pudsey

Magic

Once upon a time, there was a castle and a rainbow. There was also a dragon next to the castle. The dragon was breathing fire on the castle!
A unicorn came! The dragon and unicorn had a fight with each other.
Then it was fine and the dragon was gone.
After that, the castle was fine.

Maisy Summer Crowther (6)
Southroyd Primary School, Pudsey

Under The Sea

Once upon a time, there was a strange boat.
Under the small boat lived a friendly crab called Mr Crab.
Then a shark came to find some dinner, but the mermaid scared him off!
The mermaids had a dance party, then they said goodbye.

Lewie Ambler (5)
Southroyd Primary School, Pudsey

My Holiday

One day, I went on holiday. I lived on a boat and I fell down to the bottom of the sea where I saw a shark.

The shark looked terrible and his teeth looked sharp. A mermaid rescued us and we were safe. Mummy said thank you to the mermaid and we had a party. Then it was time to go home and we took pictures.

We said goodbye to everyone that we met and arrived home.

Angela (Yuan Yuan) Huang (5)

St Nicholas Primary School, Hull

Going On Holiday

Today I went on holiday on a boat, with Mummy and Daddy and food and drinks. Then we went to the beach.
I saw a shark in the sea. He wanted to eat me!
A mermaid saved me from the shark.
Then I was friends with the mermaid. I saw Mum and Dad on the beach.
I stayed with my mummy and daddy.

Violet Wilkinson (5)
St Nicholas Primary School, Hull

Going To The Beach

Today I went to Scarborough and I hoped it would be good.
I fell into the deep, dark sea.
A shark came to eat me but a mermaid came and flicked her tail at the shark and he swam away.
Then I was friends with the mermaid.
Then I had to go back to the beach.

Faith Dixon (5)
St Nicholas Primary School, Hull

My Holiday

One day, I went on holiday to Russia. I fell into the deep, dark sea.
The sea was somehow hot!
I saw a shark and it was fierce.
A mermaid whacked the shark with her tail.
They then laughed!
Then they got back into the boat.

Robbie West (4)
St Nicholas Primary School, Hull

Space Adventure

The rocket was going to the moon. It went too fast it went *crash!* I was in the rocket wearing a spacesuit. It crash-landed on the moon. How was I going to get home? I felt sad. I had a puppy at my house and wanted to feed it. Then a flying saucer came. I went to hide. The saucer landed and inside it was an alien! I came out. It was friendly. It used its ray to carry my rocket back home. It was very dark and I could see stars, and the moon went very fast!

The alien turned off the ray when I got home and I went inside to feed my puppy.

Liam Mpholle (7)

The Forest School, Knaresborough

In The Garden

One Friday morning, Lucas was bored so he went
into Ava's room. Lucas had a snoop for Ava's
special box, he found it and he opened it. In the
box was a special earring. Lucas touched the
earring. Before Lucas got outside, the magic began
to happen. Lucas and Ava began to shrink.
"Oh no!" said Ava. "What did you do? We'd better
get back inside before it's too late."
"Oh no! What has happened?" It was too late, they
were stuck outside.
When they were little, they saw lots of giant bugs.
One of the bugs was a bee. The bee sniffed the air.
The bee sniffed Lucas, he started to get worried.
Lucas ran.
"Oh no! Thank goodness we got away!" Lucas said,
relieved.
Another animal was an ant and the ant saw Ava
and was watching her, she whispered to Lucas.
"Oh no, why did this happen? I did not want this to
happen."
They ran to a swimming lake.
"Wow! That is really nice!" said Ava.
"I know," said Lucas, "it is like a diamond. Let's
have a swim," said Lucas.

"Yes, let's," said Ava.

They had three hours in the lake.

"Wow! That was so fun!"

"Yes, it was!"

When they got out they discovered a mountain.

"Wow! That is really big, I want to climb that," said Lucas

"Me too, let's climb it," Ava said.

"Okay," said Lucas.

"We've finally reached the top. Wow, that is a fantastic view," puffed Lucas.

"Yes, it is! I can see Floppy from up here near the jungle," said Ava.

"Also, can you see the giant strawberries? Let's get down now."

"Yes we should, before the magic stops," said Ava.

"Okay, we're down now. I feel glum because I am worried that we'll never get back to our normal selves," Ava said in a worried voice.

"I feel gloomy too, because I am so hungry!" said Lucas.

"Me too".

"Look, I can see strawberries, mmmm let's eat!" said Lucas.

"Yes, let's."

"Oh, I feel sick," said Ava.

"Me too, we need to stop eating them but I love strawberries," said Lucas, licking his lips.

"Oh no!" yelled Ava. "It is raining, we'd better get under the plant pot where we can stay dry."

"Phew! We finally made it under the plant pot," said Lucas.

Whilst they were under the plant pot, they played tig because they were bored. They could play tig under the plant pot because they were small. Within a few minutes, the rain was over and the magic was wearing off.

"Yay!" they both yelled. "Now we can go back to the sandcastle."

"Hang on a minute, when we were small there was no sandpit," Ava said.

"I know it now, the mountain was the sandcastle we made," Lucas said.

"Yeah it was, and the jungle was our grass."

"Oh yes! It makes sense now. Do you want to do it again? This time we can have fun," asked Lucas.

"No, because we may be stuck like that forever..."

Libby Louise Aston (7)
Tranmoor Primary School, Armthorpe

In The Garden

On Monday, Lexi and Leon were outside playing and Lexi crept upstairs because she knew Leon had a secret box which Lexi wasn't allowed to touch. While he wasn't in his bedroom, Lexi went and took the key. She took the key and ran outside with it and it started glowing, but suddenly, Lexi and her brother started to shrink!

Lexi and Leon could see large flowers and ants crawling.

After that, Lexi and Leon met a friendly ladybird in the grass. They went into a swimming pool and on a beach. They rode in the toy Range Rover to get down the hill.

After they rode down the hill, their next-door neighbour's cat bit their dog's puppy's tail!

After that, they started to get hungry, so they got in their dad's strawberry garden.

Suddenly, it started raining so they went into their dad's shed and locked the door so they didn't get wet. They felt a bit scared!

After, the key started glowing again so they went back to their normal size.

Lexi Challis (7)

Tranmoor Primary School, Armthorpe

In The Garden

One boring Saturday, Leah was so bored, she didn't know what to do! Then she remembered that Lyla had a golden, shiny box but she didn't know what was inside. She went upstairs and she carefully went into her sister's room. She slowly opened the box and inside was a shiny, glowing, rainbow gem.

"Lyla! Lyla!" shouted Leah.

Lyla was playing on her phone.

"What?"

Lyla put down her phone. They both began to shrink!

"What happened, Lyla?" said Leah, scared.

"First, why did you steal my gem?" shouted Lyla.

The next day, they found a lake but didn't know how to get across.

"L-Lyla, look at that millipede curled up by our feet!" shrieked Leah.

It was crawling away.

"See, it was just trying to find a place to sleep, now let's get on this cart and go home!" Lyla told Leah.

They both got to a beach.

"Wow! What a big beach!" they both shouted.

They walked and walked.

"I'm tired!" said Lyla.

"Look at those blueberries, we could eat them!" said Leah, tired.

Then Leah saw a spider.

Leah whispered to Lyla, "Look at the spider!"

"Hey, Spot's there, he could help!" said Lyla.

"Spot! Spot!" they both shouted loudly.

The spider went and they both grew back to their normal size.

Leah Nicholson (7)

Tranmoor Primary School, Armthorpe

In The Garden

One Wednesday afternoon, Ava sneakily went into her brother's room and Ava just remembered Lucas had a private, old black box and inside, a shiny golden gem. Ava carefully lifted the lid of the old box and saw the gem and the gem began to glow. Ava did not know what to do so she dashed outside to her brother, Lucas.

Suddenly, they began to shrink and they ran further into the grass. They heard a large angry dragonfly, then they reached a lake and they found a speedboat.

Lucas shouted, "This is so fast!"

But the fun was over and they reached a beach. They walked for miles and miles but then they got hotter and hotter. Then they saw a cat so they went into a bottle till Floppy chased the cat away. Then Ava and Lucas crawled out of the bottle and carried on walking. They noticed the beach was really big!

They got hot and they needed a drink. Then they found lots and lots of strawberries!

"I love strawberries!" said everyone, and they ate all of the strawberries up.

Then they felt sick! It started to rain so Ava and Lucas ran under a plant pot.

The magic gem began to glow and the magic was over. They went to normal size again. Ava had a plant pot hat.

Dad saw the strawberries eaten and he said, "There must be some big slugs around here!"

Katelyn Foers (7)

Tranmoor Primary School, Armthorpe

In The Garden

One happy Sunday, Bob was playing with Tom but Bob didn't want to play anymore.

He went into Tom's bedroom and he knew that he had a box, so he peeked behind the door to see if his mum was there. He opened the box!

In the box, there was a golden gem... The golden gem started to glow. Bob ran as fast as he could to Tom to tell him the gem was glowing. It was too late! Tom and Bob shrank! They were like tiny minibeasts and then a big bumblebee swooped down and it nearly ate Tom and Bob!

They were running like they'd never ran before. Luckily, the bumblebee was too tired.

When they got over the big hill, they saw a big, fierce, brown dog come along. He put them in a bottle!

Floppy saved them! When they got out of the bottle, they needed a drink and some food!

Eventually, they saw some strawberries. They were delighted! They nearly ate all of them!

It started to rain so Bob put a flowerpot over them so the rain didn't drip on them. The magic stopped. They grew back and the flowerpot was over Tom's head!

Dad was doing some gardening and he saw the strawberries and he said, "Are there big snails in this garden?"

Lucas Philip Cowley (6)

Tranmoor Primary School, Armthorpe

In The Garden

One Monday morning, Kacie was bored so she crept to her brother's room. She saw a ring! It was a magical ring and it started to glow. Kacie ran outside. Jayden was playing with his friends and they were playing tig. The ring was glowing.
"Run!"
But it was too late. They'd shrunk until they were the size of minibeasts!
"It's like a jungle!" said Kacie.
"It sure is! Let's go and explore!"
"Argh! A bee! Run! Phew! It was an angry bee! Phew!" said Kacie.
"Thank goodness, that was scary!"
Then they found a beach.
"Let's play!"
"Okay!" said Kacie.
After, they swam halfway and swam back.
After that, they wanted to play with toys but they couldn't find any! They searched and searched, then they found some and played.
After, they were hot. They found water and drank it until they fell asleep and snored!
One woke up and danced and woke up the other and they danced too. Then they were hungry. They found strawberries.

After two minutes, they were full! They walked home and the power stopped. They turned back to normal!

Kacie-Jayne Birtles (7)

Tranmoor Primary School, Armthorpe

In The Garden

One Sunday morning, Molly was snooping in Alice's bedroom and Molly remembered Alice had a brown box. In the box, there was a diamond! The diamond was floating, then Molly scrambled to Alice. Suddenly, Molly and Alice started to shrink and they were surrounded by tall dandelions! Then a large bumblebee came swooping down and tried to eat them! Then they climbed up a hill and they found a toy boat. They rowed across the lake and when they got across, a car threw them in a bottle! "Floppy! Away!" Molly said. "Good old Floppy!" They reached into the strawberries and ate them. Molly said, "I feel sick!"

"Me too!" said Alice.

It started to rain. They hid under the plant pot, then the spell broke.

Alice said, "I like your new hat!"

Then their dad found out that someone had eaten the strawberries!

Olivia Jane Watkinson (7)
Tranmoor Primary School, Armthorpe

In The Garden

One Wednesday morning, Flynn was bored, so he decided to go upstairs. Flynn crept into his brother's room because he knew that he had a golden box and inside was a magic wand. The wand started to glow so he ran outside to tell his brothers. They were too late and they started to shrink.

Flynn and Sam shrunk into the grass and they saw a bumblebee, so they ran away from it.

When they reached the end of the grass, they saw a hill but it was a sandpit and they were thinking how to get down the hill. They found a toy car and when they reached the bottom of the hill, a cat came along and nearly tried to eat them!

The boys ran into a hotel, then they saw strawberries and it started to rain. After that, the wand started to fade and they started to grow and Dad was confused.

He pulled a face and said, "I am sure the caterpillars have been eating!"

Flynn White (7)

Tranmoor Primary School, Armthorpe

In The Garden

One sunny morning, Dasi was in Milo's bedroom. Dasi knew that under Milo's bed was an old, green box. She grabbed the box sneakily and looked back to see if her mum was there. Inside the old, green box there was a shiny, golden ring. It started to glow!

She said, "Oh no! I've got to tell Milo! He is only outside!" She ran outside and told her brother but it was too late! They shrunk into the long, green grass and started to explore. When they got to the desert, they saw a big, big cat and they jumped into a bottle. Floppy the dog chased the cat away and they all jumped out of the bottle. They explored some more.

Dasi said, "I am hungry!"

They went to a bunch of blueberries and chomped and chomped until they were full up. They ran under a plant pot and then the magic went away!

Ava Rose Barrass (7)
Tranmoor Primary School, Armthorpe

In The Garden

One cold afternoon, Olly snuck into his brother's bedroom and looked under his brother's bed. He saw a big private box and a key was inside the box so Olly ran outside quickly, but it was too late. They started to shrink, so Olly and Finley crawled through the grass and they saw an ant and a bumblebee!

An hour later, Olly and Finley found a Jeep so they jumped into the Jeep. When Olly and Finley got to the top of the mountain, they spotted an angry spider coming towards them! They hid in the grass but they were hungry, so they started to eat some strawberries.

Two minutes later, it started to rain. Olly and Finley started to feel sick and the magic was over.

"At last! I didn't like the forest!" said Olly. "I didn't like the angry spider because it tried to eat us!"

Bradley Wehrle (7)

Tranmoor Primary School, Armthorpe

In The Garden

One sunny day, Bob was bored, but he remembered Frank had a black Coke bottle. He opened the lid and there was a lizard key ring and lizards shot out of the key rings. The key ring started to glow so he ran outside to his brother, Frank, but it was too late! They got smaller until they were minibeast size!

"Wow! These flowers are magic!" screamed Bob. Suddenly, a gigantic ladybird flew over and tried to eat them, so they climbed up a rocky hill. They saw a jet ski! They went down a waterfall and a crocodile tried to eat them. A raft went down the waterfall and hit the crocodile. They felt excited! They got off the jet ski and they saw some apples so they pulled big blobs off.

The children ate them and their dad said, "These bugs have been eating the apples!"

Niall Nevin (7)
Tranmoor Primary School, Armthorpe

In The Garden

One Sunday afternoon Greg had nothing to do, so he thought, *why not snoop in Edd's room?*
Then Greg just remembered that Edd had a pirate box and inside was a ruby. The ruby began to glow and Greg and Edd shrank to the size of a minibeast! In fact, even smaller!
Greg and Edd were in the grass.
"What huge flowers!" cried Edd.
"Run!" shouted Greg.
An army of ants were crawling towards them. Greg and Edd ran for cover! They were so hungry.
"I'm hungry!" said Greg.
"Look!" said Edd. "Giant cherries! I love cherries!"
"Me too!" said Greg.
Then the magic began to stop. Mum looked at the cherries. "They must be giant slugs!" she said.

Harry Walker (7)

Tranmoor Primary School, Armthorpe

In The Garden

One Friday morning, Libby was bored so she went into Leah's room and found a box. She carefully lifted the lid of the box. In it was a magic wand! The wand started to glow. Libby ran outside. She told Leah.

Leah said, "Get inside!"

The wand began to work.

"Oh, what can we do?

"Let's see, come on!" said Leah.

"Let's climb up this hill. Wow! Let's go back down."

"Wow! A toy car! Let's get in!"

"It's cool! Get in! Let's go fast!"

"Argh! A car! Run! Hurry!

"I have found a glass, let's get in it!" Leah said.

Mason Walker (6)
Tranmoor Primary School, Armthorpe

In The Garden

One sunny morning, Sam went into his brother's room and got a box. He looked inside the box and found a magical key! Sam picked up the box and the key began to glow.

Sam ran outside to tell his brother, Tom. Tom was cross because Sam went into his room! The key was still glowing and they boys were the size of minibeasts. They saw a huge caterpillar and saw lots of bugs and they were eating leaves! They were scared that the bugs were going to eat them. The magic started to wear off and they were becoming big again. It was much better than being small!

Fletcher Elden (7)

Tranmoor Primary School, Armthorpe

In The Garden

One Sunday morning, Faith went into her sister's bedroom. Faith remembered she had a pink box. Then she opened it. It had a shiny key. She picked it up and the key started to glow. Then Faith ran to Lilly to tell her that the key was glowing. Suddenly, they shrunk into the grass. Then they went into the grass. A grasshopper came and Faith and Lily went into the house. Then they went back outside. They helped each other. Faith and Lilly were happy but hungry! They went to the hot tub and pool because they were hot.

Faith Doherty (7)
Tranmoor Primary School, Armthorpe

In The Garden

One sunny morning, Tom found a box and inside the box was a key. The key was magic! Tom went to tell his brother, Sam, and Sam was cross.

They began to shrink to the size of a spider! They climbed the golden treasure chest because a boulder was rolling towards them. They were terrified! A giant ant carried the boulder back to the rocky hillside and Tom and Sam were safe! They found the magic wore off and they grew back to normal size. They were grateful because they didn't like being small!

Flynn Broome (6)

Tranmoor Primary School, Armthorpe

In The Garden

One sunny morning, Sam went into his brother's room and got a box. He looked inside the box and found a magical key! The key began to glow. The boys began to shrink. They were underneath tall, wavy grass and felt a bit worried because they didn't know what was going to happen! A buzzing bee flew onto a tall flower next to them.

Then the magic began to wear off and everything was back to normal. They were over the moon once they were big again!

James Grey (7)
Tranmoor Primary School, Armthorpe

In The Garden

One Saturday morning, Tom sneaked into Madi's room and found a dusty, old box. Inside was a blue ring. It began to glow! Madi and Tom went into the grass and could see a sunflower hanging above their heads. Then they found a dragonfly and the car killed it. Then they found a lake and a beach. Then they went down and felt sad. Then the magic ended and they were happy.

Dylan Marshall (7)
Tranmoor Primary School, Armthorpe

The Sparkly Mermaid

I had to go on a rowing boat and I stopped in the middle of the light blue ocean. I put my anchor down and jumped off the boat.

I swam to the bottom of the deep ocean. The ocean was dark and spooky!

I found a grey cave and it had water icicles.

A mermaid came out of the cave. The mermaid's tail was sparkly pink and then she saw a mean shark!

She grabbed my hand and pulled me to the side. She put some shark food in the cave and the shark went to eat the food. The mermaid trapped it with a big, big rock!

Me and the mermaid swam to the top of the ocean. I copied the mermaid and I felt safer.

Elaina-Mai Petch (5)

West End Academy, Hemsworth

The Blue Submarine

I set off for Spain in my blue submarine with metal patches. I looked out of the window and I looked at the stripy clownfish and the anglerfish. I looked out of my telescope and I saw some grey rocks. Then a friendly pufferfish came out of the rocks and said, "Hi!"

A killer whale was swimming and his big tail whacked off my telescope and I couldn't see. I did not know where to go.

Soon, I was in South America.

Ivy Clough (5)

West End Academy, Hemsworth

The Mermaids And The Sharks

The mermaids were playing with a treasure chest in their cave. The sharks tried to get in. The mermaids slammed the door right in their faces! The mermaids and fish had a lovely party and they dressed up in their party. They had balloons, cake and celebration presents.

They won and the sad sharks went back into the deep, deep cave.

Holly Camponi (5)

West End Academy, Hemsworth

The Gold Treasure

I went on a pirate submarine to find gold treasure. I wore a scuba costume. I swam down to a broken shipwreck. The treasure was there. There was a shark attack and a purple octopus came and it tangled me up in its tentacles. I chopped them off with a waterproof hook. I took my treasure to the submarine.

Kye Julian Stogden (5)
West End Academy, Hemsworth

Deadly Draper

There was a pony called Sparky, who lived a lovely life in a field and she was owned by a little girl called Megan. Sparky loved an adventure and unbeknown to Megan and her family, she went on many adventures! Sparky liked to escape into the forests to go and eat the magic bark on the trees. The bark gave Sparky magical powers that turned her into a unicorn.

She went further along the forest when she saw the most beautiful rainbow over the castle. However, this worried Sparky as a rainbow was a sign that her help was needed and fast!

The evil dragon called Draper had been flying over the forest, looking for something to eat, when all of a sudden, he could smell food. He could smell humans! Draper saw a little girl playing outside. Draper, the nasty dragon, turned and flew down to get the little princess. He thought there was a chance!

Luckily, the queen called for the princess to come inside for her lunch.

Draper the dragon was very angry and very hungry. He was so cross, he stood on his back legs and breathed the hot, yellow fire out of his mouth towards the castle.

Draper's vicious eyes flickered as he blew a fireball out of his mouth. Sparky cantered as fast as she could go towards the castle.

Suddenly, Sparky saw the stinky dragon breathing his fire towards the castle, so Sparky the magical unicorn used all the power she had in her horn and shot magic at Draper and his fire.

Draper could not fight off Sparky's magic powers. He tried but they were just too strong for him. He spread his gigantic wings and with all his might, pushed himself into the sky and flew far, far away back into the mountains.

Sparky was so pleased she had been there to protect the lovely royal family, however, it was starting to become night-time and she knew that Megan would be coming to see her.

Sparky cantered again as fast as she could up the lane and back into her field, and turned back into a pony before anyone knew about her skill of turning into a unicorn and her escaping adventure.

Megan Pearson (7)
Woodlands CE Primary School, Woodlands

Under The Sea

Once upon a time, there was a boy called Bob. One day, Bob got in his boat and rowed to the middle of the ocean. He stopped for a while as he was exhausted! Whilst he was resting, he saw some beautiful coral and fish. He put on his wetsuit and snorkel and got on the edge of the boat and dived in to look closer.

There were some tiny fish and gigantic fish! They were all different colours like a rainbow.

As Bob was looking at the coral, he suddenly saw a shark! He was terrified!

Thankfully, a beautiful mermaid and her dad showed up and scared the shark away.

Bob said, "Thank you!" to the mermaid as he looked at her dreamily.

He was very glad she had turned up. Bob decided it was time to go home. He swam back to his boat and got in.

As he started to row, he turned and waved goodbye to the mermaid and her dad.

Harry Mitchell (6)
Woodlands CE Primary School, Woodlands

Jungle

Once, there was a dark, gloomy and scary woods. Inside was a scary snake. He hissed at me and I was terrified! He was unhappy and he hissed so loud, I nearly became deaf! Then I saw his sharp, pointy teeth.

Then a friendly lion came and I said to him, "What should we play?"

He said, "Let's race!"

We did and of course, he was first but one round he let me win because he was tired.

Then my mum called for me because it was tea time and I told my mum all about it.

Austin Wade (7)

Woodlands CE Primary School, Woodlands

Underwater Adventure

I left home to go on an adventure across the sea. I dived down deep into the sea and looked at all the fish. Just then, I met a crab and it said hello! This was very strange.

Then a shark swam towards us. We were very scared! A mermaid and king mermaid saw what happened and came to help us. They chased the naughty shark away.

We were all very happy that the shark was gone. I swam back to my boat and waved goodbye to my new friends.

Then I woke up! What an amazing dream.

Lily Ford (7)
Woodlands CE Primary School, Woodlands

The Castle And The Dragon

A long time ago, there was a great, big castle. A princess lived in the castle.

One day, a dragon came to the castle. He went to the gates and then he had an idea! The dragon's idea was to burn the castle. He breathed fire on the castle.

Then the dragon met a unicorn. The unicorn pushed the dragon. The dragon flew away. He was never seen again!

It was night-time and the unicorn went to bed. The princess lived happily ever after.

Eva Lee (6)

Woodlands CE Primary School, Woodlands

Under The Sea

On one sunny day, there was a little boat floating on the sea. Then it was about to float away under the sea. There was a happy, little, pinchy crab and with the crab were fish.

Just then, a shark appeared and frightened the crab into his shell. The sea king was going to save the mermaid, then the shark went away.

The mermaid and merking were dancing around. The mermaid and the merking were so happy that they had smiles on their faces.

Olivia Brooke Atkins (7)
Woodlands CE Primary School, Woodlands

Under The Sea

Once upon a time, a rowing boat was out at sea.
Under the sea lived a crab and his friends. They all
enjoyed playing together.
One day, a ginormous, scary shark crept up on the
crab. The crab was so scared, he screamed!
Far away, the mermaids heard his scream and
rushed to help! The mermaids cheered as they
managed to save him. They were all very happy!
The mermaids waved goodbye to the crab, then
they swam home!

Isabelle Johnson (6)

Woodlands CE Primary School, Woodlands

Under The Sea

I rowed my boat out on an adventure. I saw some colourful fish and strange creatures. An angry, big shark came to eat me up!

Neptune and a pretty mermaid chased the scary shark away. We had a disco with lots of dancing sparkly seahorses.

I waved goodbye and I said, "I love you, see you soon!"

Scarlet Tempest (6)

Woodlands CE Primary School, Woodlands

Unicorn Saves The Day

Once upon a time, there was a castle. The castle was pink, blue and purple. A dragon tried to set the castle on fire and he did set the castle on fire. A unicorn came and saved everyone! The unicorn made the dragon fly off! Then the unicorn went back to her house, tired.

Rosie Elizabeth Swift (7)
Woodlands CE Primary School, Woodlands

Back In Time!

Once upon a time, a boy called Greg built a time machine.
Greg met some dinosaurs. Some dinosaurs were nice, some dinosaurs were mean.
Greg found a nest with eggs in.
The eggs had baby pterodactyls in!
Greg went home and sold his time machine.

James Turkmen Holmes (7)
Woodlands CE Primary School, Woodlands

The Storyboards

Here are the fun storyboards
children could choose from...

Jungle

Magical

Under the Sea

Space

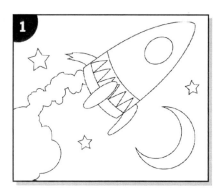

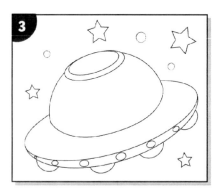

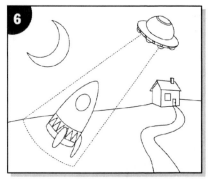

Dinosaur

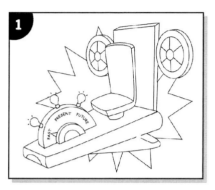

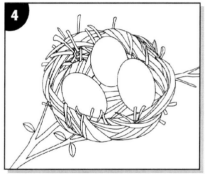

First published in Great Britain in 2018 by:

Young Writers
Remus House
Coltsfoot Drive
Peterborough
PE2 9BF
Telephone: 01733 890066
Website: www.youngwriters.co.uk

Young Writers
Information

We hope you have enjoyed reading this book and
that you will continue to in the coming years.

If you're a young writer who enjoys reading and creative
writing, or the parent of an enthusiastic poet or story writer,
do visit our website **www.youngwriters.co.uk**. Here you
will find free competitions, workshops and games, as well
as recommended reads, a poetry glossary and our blog.

If you would like to order further copies of this book, or any of
our other titles give us a call or visit **www.youngwriters.co.uk**.

Young Writers
Remus House
Coltsfoot Drive
Peterborough
PE2 9BF

(01733) 890066
info@youngwriters.co.uk